She began kissing me over and over. "Veronica, come with me on a dream journey!"

Her warm hands interlocked with mine. She kissed my lips, my eyes, my cheeks. Lightly, she nipped my chin then my neck. Gently licking, her hot tongue flicked warmth across my shoulder. She grasped my hands tighter.

"Say yes, Veronica. Please, Veronica." Her words were muffled, less distinct.

She sucked my tender skin into her mouth and a hot current surged from her to me. Every nerve ending buzzed frantically. Trembling waves rose.

My nipples tightened as if a live wire were stimulating them unmercifully. Her knowing mouth moved closer. As if we had always been lovers, as if it had always been this way, I unbuttoned my shirt for her.

Beet-red, my nipples were desperately hard. And she knew, oh she knew. Teasing the areolas, she flicked with her warm tongue. The smooth pink contracted into rouge-waved flesh. My nipples ached. I forced her mouth to me and begged her to suck.

"Please, Amanda. Please." As if we had always been lovers, as if it had always been this way, I pleaded.

I pressed my body to hers. She pressed hers to mine. The pressure of her hipbone against my mound was direct. Rocking, grinding, she rode me . . .

About the Author

Robbi Sommers was born in Cincinnati, Ohio in 1950. She lives in Northern California where she divides her time between Dental Hygiene, motherhood and writing. The author of the best-selling erotica *Pleasures, Players, Kiss and Tell, Behind Closed Doors, Personal Ads,* and *Getting There* she shyly admits to "liking a good time."

Uncertain

COMPANIONS

ROBBI SOMMERS

The Naiad Press, Inc.
1997

Printed in the United States of America on acid-free paper
First Edition
Second Printing, August 1994
Third Printing, April 1997

Edited by Christine Cassidy
Cover design by Pat Tong and Bonnie Liss
    (Phoenix Graphics)
Typeset by Sandi Stancil

Library of Congress Cataloging-in-Publication Data

Sommers, Robbi, 1950–
    Uncertain companions / by Robbi Sommers.
        p.   cm.
    ISBN 1-56280-017-5
    I. Title.
PS3569.065335U5   1992
813'.54—dc20   92-20803
                                                              CIP

Into the world of illusions, I was swept ...
In memory of the dreams

Thank you for inspiration:

Barbara Walker's: *Women's Encyclopedia
of Myths and Secrets*
Barbara Walker's: *The Women's Dictionary —
Symbols and Sacred Objects*
The women who have brought me dreams
My muse who knows . . .

Amanda no longer takes the dream journeys. She says, under no circumstances would she try it again. I believe her ... but I've burned the book and tossed those damn dream bags in the trash anyway. I will not take chances.

Those who have chased dreams sooner or later are compelled to seek again. Feronia taught me that lesson. But the cautious know to be wary. Uncertain paths lead to uncertain companions and I have no time for that.

From the journals of Veronica

Veronica:
The Kiss

Chapter 1

I had expected the day to be ordinary; dull really. After several years as a dental hygienist, work was predictable. At seven-forty-five, Karen and I reviewed the day's schedule over coffee. At eight, the patients arrived.

Until Amanda, this morning had been no different than yesterday or the day before. The usual forenoon fog draped the courtyard like a thick lace veil. Swollen orange-yellow buds, thick on green bushes, patiently awaited the sun's caress. Nine o'clock, ten o'clock, my clients came and went.

I stared into the courtyard. While I had been cleaning teeth, the flowers had exploded into burnt-orange and yellows. Like full-skirted dancers, the ball-gown petals reached for the noon-hour light. Bees soared over the fence, splashed into the satin fragrance and flitted out of sight.

Ten minutes had passed since my eleven o'clock patient had been dismissed, yet the compelling scent she wore still lingered. An interesting blend — honeysuckle and pine? — seemed to envelop me like the silky midday flowers did the bees.

Amanda. Amanda Cartel. Earlier, coffee cup in hand, Karen had referred to this very woman. "You're seeing a lipstick lez today." She pointed to the eleven slot.

"A what?" I glanced at the small typed letters.

"You know," Karen replied, teasingly. "A lipstick lez. A femme lesbian."

"Yeah, and how do you know she's a lesbian?" I said with a laugh.

"Because she's an old friend of mine." Karen smiled.

"How close a friend?" I whispered with implication.

"About as close as you and I." She winked.

Amanda, the lipstick lez, arrived on time. So what, a mouth was a mouth, lipstick lez or not. I expected a routine teeth-cleaning and nothing more. But as Amanda rose from the reception room chair, as her forest breeze swirled down the hallway, I felt a peculiar sense of interest. Her autumn-colored skirt, like wind-spun gauze, hung full to mid-calf. A

4

melody of tiny clinks accompanied her movements and I imagined silver-charmed bracelets strung around her ankle.

I had never met a lesbian before, at least not that I had been aware of. Even though Karen had said lipstick, what did I know? I anticipated short hair, jeans and a flannel shirt. With her green-shadowed eyes, her tumbling hair, the beaded earrings and the calf-length skirt, Amanda — lipstick or not — was not what I would have expected.

Her dark hair, black as moonless midnight, richly contrasted her creamy complexion. Depending on the lighting, her eyes shaded into grays, blues, and violets. As I cleaned her teeth, I would occasionally adjust the overhead light, just to see her eyes react.

One front top tooth, slightly overlapping the other, added an interesting imperfection to her runaway smile. She had an inexplicable magnetism — was it her eyes, mysterious yet promising? Her words, understated yet precise? — whatever, Amanda, with woodsy scents and enigmatic eyes, had something, something I wanted, yet I had no idea what it could be.

I wondered: if Karen hadn't mentioned anything to me, would I have been so intrigued? As I sat next to Amanda and studied her mouth, I speculated about the things, the unknown things, that women like her must do.

I had never considered kissing, let alone making love, to another woman. But there was something decidedly compelling about a woman who had.

Not that we discussed such things. Absolutely

not. The conversation had been entirely chitchat. Even so, as I watched the bees dive into honeyed oblivion, I had the perplexing sensation that we had spoken of much, much more.

Chapter 2

Less than a week later, over lunch at our favorite restaurant, Karen turned to me and casually asked, "Remember that woman, Amanda Cartel? She was a patient of yours."

"Amanda Cartel?" I said nonchalantly, although the very mention of her name triggered an immediate response deep within.

"The lipstick lez," Karen said with a smile.

"Oh yeah, sure, I remember her," I said evenly. I concentrated on stirring the bowl of hot soup before me.

"She called me last night," Karen continued. "She wanted to know about you."

"Me?" I watched the thin noodles swirl in the broth.

"Yeah, you." There was a teasing edge to Karen's words. "She wondered if you'd be interested in going out with her."

"Me?" I said again, not lifting my spoon from the soup.

"I told her you were married." Karen was talking quickly, oblivious to the effect of her own words. "And she said, 'That doesn't answer my question. What I asked is if you think she'd be interested in having dinner with me.'" Karen tapped her spoon against my hand. "Can you beat that?"

Karen and I often ate lunch together. We'd walk to the Chinese restaurant down the street, slide into our regular corner booth and immerse ourselves in a quick round of what we called bullshit-lunch-talk.

As usual, Karen was in routine gossip mode. But this time I was unusually engrossed in what she was saying. Each word about Amanda seemed important. Each implication felt mysteriously significant.

"So then I said," Karen tapped my hand again as if to ensure my attention, "'Veronica is *very* heterosexual.'" Karen laughed. "Very heterosexual. How's that! After all, a woman like you — well, I think very heterosexual sums it up, don't you?"

I nodded, not quite able to speak.

"An affair, well maybe. But *you* and a woman?" Karen quipped. "I think not!"

There was a gnawing, hollow sensation in my stomach. I had a vision of myself in a small red car slowly climbing the highest peak of a roller coaster track. I felt charged with unfamiliar anticipation.

"I don't see any harm in dinner." I sipped my soup as though indifferent, then flashed Karen a no-big-deal smile. After all, it wasn't a big deal. Amanda was an interesting, vivacious woman. The fact that she was a lesbian had no relevance. An evening with an engaging person, a person Jason wouldn't regard as a threat, seemed like a delightful idea. It would be nice to have an evening out without Jason's jealousies.

Karen placed her spoon on the table. "You want to go out with her?" she asked incredulously.

"I'm not interested in her like *that*," I said defensively. "Amanda seems very insightful, very thought-provoking. I could use a person like that in my life right now."

Insightful? Thought-provoking? My own words surprised me. I hadn't the slightest idea if Amanda was either.

"Of course you're not interested in her *like that*." Karen had returned to her bullshit-lunch-talk mode. "Amanda's a great person, yes, and very insightful. She's a good friend to have."

"Yes, a friend," I repeated, lost in thought. What was it about Amanda that interested me? What exactly was I seeking?

I broke open my fortune cookie and unraveled the thin paper.

"Looks like I'm going on a journey." Karen tossed her fortune on the table.

"Yeah, me too."

* * * * *

I tried to be blasé, but the next day I was unnaturally consumed with interest in the telephone. Each time it rang, unexpected anxiety shot through me. Hoping it was her, but not knowing why I hoped, I waited.

When Amanda finally called, I was flustered. She, on the other hand, sounded carefree and vivacious as though we had spoken countless times before.

"Karen gave me your home number, I trust that's okay," Amanda said. Did she sense my nervousness?

"Oh, of course." I was talking, I know that, but exactly what I was saying, I wasn't sure. I could hardly hear my own voice — what with the sound of my heart racing, what with my body feeling so afloat. I was here but I wasn't here at all.

Even on the phone, the connection I felt was potent. Amanda had a magic about her, a subtle heat, a curious vividness.

". . . so I thought we could meet at Joe's Pasta Bar on Friday." Her voice seemed to whirl with the offer of unlimited possibilities.

"Dinner. Yes, sounds great!" Was that me speaking? Was it her? Things were spinning.

She made a quick joke, laughed, then said she'd see me on Friday.

I hung up and stared out the kitchen window at the large oak tree. Amanda's energy transfixed me. Compared to my vague emptiness, she seemed saturated with life. I was idle and she was charged. She was the journey and I, a hapless traveler.

"Veronica?" Jason's voice brought me from my daze.

I wrote Amanda's name in thick red letters on

the calendar then returned to the den. Jason's cocktail was half consumed.

"Who was that on the phone?" he asked. He didn't turn from the television.

"Amanda." I peered at Vanna White as she turned the letter *T*.

After dinner was Jason's time to relax. A man whose days were filled with business maneuvers and constant stress, Jason was specific about his routine.

"I like two martinis," Jason had said when we first started dating, two and a half years before. "Two martinis and the *Wheel of Fortune*. Don't ask me to think when I get home." And true to his word, when Jason got home, he stopped thinking.

I looked at him. With his strong build, his dark, *GQ* looks, his money — I knew that many women envied me. I had it all yet had nothing.

"Who did you say?"

"Amanda Cartel." I repeated her name. I liked her name, the way the letters rolled on my tongue. "She asked me to dinner Friday evening. We don't have plans, do we?"

Jason brought the glass to his lips. "Amanda Cartel?" He turned toward me. I could already anticipate the questions.

"A woman I met at work. Dinner, that's all, just dinner."

"No dancing? No nightclub after?" Jason's voice was low, quiet. Even though one year had passed since the affair, he still worried where I was going and with whom.

"This woman is a lesbian, Jason. She's a good friend of Karen's. We're having dinner. I'm sure that the last place she'd want to go is a straight dance club."

"And you? Is that the last place *you'd* like to go?" Jason said, a thin edge to his voice. After all, isn't that where I had met Jonathan? Isn't that where it had all started?

I walked over to Jason and rested my hand on his shoulder. "Just dinner, Jason. With a woman that I can guarantee won't be interested in flirting with men."

Just dinner. How casual those words seemed. Dinner with a lesbian, a lipstick lez. Nothing more.

Jason touched my waist tentatively. "I can't help if I worry, Veronica. After all we've been through."

"Yes, of course." I sighed.

Turning to the TV, Jason handed me his glass. "How about a refill?"

Chapter 3

Dinner had gone remarkably fast, or so it seemed. Amanda's anecdotes of her days in the Army held my interest, yet the undercurrent between us made complete concentration difficult.

"I don't know." Amanda swirled a spaghetti noodle on her fork. "I was just a buck-ass private. But before I knew it, I found myself in bed with the drill sergeant."

I watched intently as she sucked the dangling noodle into her mouth.

"Don't get me wrong," she laughed. "It's not that

I didn't know I was attracted to women. I just didn't have any real opportunities until Lillian opened the door for me. Back then, it was difficult for lesbians to find one another."

"And today it's easier?" I watched Amanda lick the last bit of tomato sauce from her fork.

"Things are more open these days, but even so, I've developed a sixth sense about women. When I look into a woman's eyes, sometimes it's just there, I can feel it. Know what I mean?" She looked directly into my eyes.

I was filled with a sudden anxiety. What was she implying? How could *I* possibly know what she meant? Searching another woman's eyes, sensing that sort of thing with a woman — this was an area where I certainly had no experience.

Attempting to break the stronghold of her straightforward gaze, I watched her lips. Her glossy-red lipstick dramatized their fullness. In striking contrast, her white teeth glimmered like expensive pearls.

I glanced back to her eyes. What was it about this woman that fascinated me? It wasn't sexual, I argued to myself. I couldn't now, or ever, imagine myself touching another woman in that way. It didn't make sense. What possible pay-off was there in woman-to-woman sex? And even if such an idea were to occur to me, even if for some crazy reason I did consider kissing Amanda, placing my lips on hers —

"Would you like dessert or are you ready to leave?" Amanda said. The tip of her tongue lightly wet the borders of her mouth.

Every word seemed to lift from her lips and float

14

to my ears. I liked her. I liked the way she had talked about herself, her astute sense of who she was and where she was heading. I envied her blatant independence.

In my own life, I felt confined, like a prisoner. I cared for Jason. Our home was beautiful and I had everything. Yet I was occasionally haunted by a vague longing. A quiet desperation shadowed my every move — like hunger, like a gnawing emptiness — it was always there. Even with everything, I had nothing. The affair with Jonathan had been a disastrous attempt to escape. But to where?

In Amanda's eyes, hidden in their deep purple hue, I imagined the night sky. Secrets, laden with promises of abandon, seemed to swirl in their darkness. As I sat with Amanda, watched Amanda, listened to Amanda, I had a strange sensation that she held the key.

After dinner, Amanda suggested a walk. The brisk night, lit only by dim street lamps, whispered with anticipation. The night air flirted with my face and teased my hands as the winter wind coaxed me forward.

Amanda took my hand. My initial response, to casually let my hand fall out of hers, was short-lived. Instead, feeling quite tentative, I looked straight ahead and kept my pace. Neither of us spoke.

When we returned to my car, Amanda, in a quick movement, embraced me. "I had a wonderful time tonight," she whispered. She held me tighter. "From the first moment I saw you, I had a sense of destiny."

Until recently, the idea of a woman whispering in

my ear as she embraced me seemed inconceivable, but tonight it felt oddly natural. Amanda's perfume, this time a light floral scent, evoked images of yellows and pinks of a summer field. Surrounded by her colorful warmth, I felt protected from the cold winter night. Her heat was mysteriously inviting and seemed to flow into me. An overwhelming desire to stay in her arms swept through me.

"Are you working tomorrow?" She brushed a rebel curl from my forehead.

I shook my head.

"Then I'll call you at home. That is okay, isn't it? It won't cause problems if I call you at home?" Her voice was subdued.

"Why would it cause problems?" I searched her starless-night eyes. "It's not as if —"

"Oh, but it *is* as if," Amanda interrupted. Her cool fingertip traced my lips in a light caress. "As far as I'm concerned, it's very much as if."

"But I —"

Amanda's lovely lips, alighting on mine, quickly silenced me. She moved her warm tongue between my lips and into my mouth. Her fragrance enveloped me like a morning fog. She hesitated as though waiting for my reaction and then gently eased further in. Her lips were like clouds, only more plush; like expensive silks, only more fine; like exotic flower petals, only smoother. I fell into a flurry of cherry blossoms. There was nothing like her kiss. Nothing. A caring, a gentleness, a quiet understanding — unlike anything I had ever before experienced — passed between us. No, there was nothing like Amanda's kiss — strong, yet very, very soft.

* * * * *

When I opened the front door, I was relieved to find that Jason had already retired for the evening. I poured a drink and sat in the darkness considering my situation.

After Jonathan, Jason and I had agreed upon complete honesty. Even if I flirted with the idea of an affair, I had promised I would talk to Jason first. But Amanda's kiss was certainly not the prelude to an affair. Clearly a mere display of affection, it was a simple, harmless kiss.

I would just tell him . . . I would just tell him . . .

"Veronica?" Jason clicked on the light. "Did you have a good time?" Wrapped in a satin comforter, he crossed the room to his easy chair.

I had a fleeting hope that he'd turn on the TV, but he directed himself to me. "I wasn't certain if I heard you come in. Why are you sitting here in the dark?"

"I assumed you were asleep." I tried to conceal my desire to be alone. I walked to his side and touched his hand. He was warm. The comforter was warm. The entire picture was warm. I felt suddenly chilled.

"I had a very nice time." I pressed a corner of the deep green comforter between my fingers. Soft and plush. I thought of Amanda's mouth. "She's an interesting woman."

"And after dinner, after she left?"

"Jason," I said evenly. "I came directly home."

"Now that's the kind of friendship I like," Jason said with a relieved smile. In his dark brown eyes, I could find no suggestion of the promises that Amanda's had held.

Deciding not to mention the kiss, I smiled sweetly.

Chapter 4

Amanda called the next morning, to say hello, to see if I was enjoying the rain. I was. The continual downpour provided a perfect backdrop for my overcast mood.

Since last night, Amanda's soft kiss had preoccupied me. As if her moist lips had been anointed with an enchanting elixir, one kiss and I was bewitched. From her lips to mine, a charged excitement had passed and I was besieged with a curious sense of hope.

The kiss confused me. Did I desire her? Certainly

not — I wasn't a lesbian. Yet one kiss and a spiraling tiny flame had been sparked. What the heat meant, why it wouldn't stop, I had no clue.

As the kiss shadowed me, my sense of disloyalty simmered. How could I explain the kiss to Jason when I was so perplexed myself? Glowing secrets — I had kissed a woman. Red hot secrets — I had kissed a woman. My emotions were in turmoil.

I watched the rain hit the sidewalk then splash toward the cloud-laden sky. It was a day to stay inside and relish the shelter.

"Will you meet me for coffee? Do you mind coming out in the rain?" Amanda's voice on the phone brought me back from my thoughts.

"Oh, I don't mind the rain," I said, still staring out the window, certain that it was more than a winter storm I was about to enter.

Amanda was already at the crowded café when I arrived. I had no difficulty finding her. The patrons blurred into a colored maze of which Amanda was the center.

An electricity leapt across the room when her eyes first met mine. I walked toward her, my heart racing. Did I smell her perfume? I thought so. Could I taste her lips? I thought so. Like a light-desperate moth, one moment I was on the opposite side of the room and the next I was in the heat.

Amanda's dark hair seemed blacker. Her ruby lips, redder. She had shadowed her eyes in gray as though coordinating with the rain. Black eyeliner, thinly penciled beneath her lashes, enhanced her exotic look. Her eyes, now a dark purplish-gray, seemed to have changed with the weather, altered with the mood.

The V-cut of her black wool sweater exposed pale skin. I lingered momentarily on the hint of her full breasts, then drifted to the strands of multi-colored beads that twisted into a thick necklace. Once again, I was in thrall.

I sat down and the smoothness of her voice relaxed and excited me all at once. Her rainbow words matched the colors of her necklace. They seemed to twirl then break into crystal prisms with her light laughter.

Amanda talked about her poetry; I thought about her kiss. She talked about her garden; I thought about her kiss. She talked about football; I thought about her kiss.

"Do you like football? We could watch the game at my house. Or do you have to get home?" Amanda glanced at her watch.

Football? I hated football. The mention of football brought forth visions of Jason, at home, glued to the set. There was nothing appealing about returning to that. Yet there was something wonderfully inviting about football with Amanda.

"I love football," I smiled.

Amanda lived on the outskirts of town. Heavy fog blanketed the country roads. The farther we traveled, the deeper into the mist I drove, following the red taillights of Amanda's car. In the rear view mirror was a hazy gray curtain. Nothing behind me, leaving one world and entering another, I trailed Amanda down a gravel road to an old, white house.

With its ivy-covered porch, its creaking wooden swing, the house stood in the mist like a small haven. I climbed from the car. The scent of eucalyptus and anise swirled in the crisp air. The cool, drizzling rain misted my face. I looked forward to Amanda and what lay ahead.

The screened front door opened directly into a sitting room where a red Victorian couch, flanked by two dark-upholstered chairs, stood before a stone fireplace. Potted plants, filling the entire length of mantle, created a green border for the rectangular mirror that hung above.

Large Oriental rugs, deep reds and dark blues, partially covered the hardwood floors in both the sitting room and small dining area off to the right. On the dining table, pewter candlesticks housed half-burned black candles. Hardened melted wax dripped from the holders like black icicles.

"It's nice here." I touched a candle tentatively and walked over to a tall bookcase against the wall.

"I love the country. I don't think I could ever return to the suburbs after living here." Amanda clicked on a beaded floor lamp and golden light flooded the room.

I ran my fingertip along the books crammed on the bookshelf. *The Scarlet Letter.* How long since I had read that? Carl Jung's *Dreams and Reflections.* *The I Ching.* *The Women's Encyclopedia of Myths and Secrets.* Joyce Carol Oates.

"An interesting mix of books." I glanced at Amanda.

"Love to read." She swept ashes from the

fireplace with a hand broom. "Love to escape into somebody else's world."

Escape. I certainly knew about that. I peeked out the tapestry-curtained window to the small fenced back yard. The cloudy mist still hung low. Amanda's house, secreted in dreamlike fog, offered escape.

Next to an oak-paneled hallway that opened into a kitchen, a free-standing beveled mirror reflected my image. Surrounded by the light's golden haze, I appeared to waver, as though fading. I stared, overcome with an eerie sensation that my image was disappearing into the glass to another era. The sudden sound of the television broke the momentary illusion.

"Just started," Amanda said as she threw a large floppy rain hat over her charcoal-colored hair. "Make yourself comfortable. I'll get some wood for a fire." She hurried out the front door, the screen door slamming behind her.

My curious fascination for Amanda extended to her house as well. Her decor wove present into past. Atop a lace-covered end table, an array of silver-framed photographs surrounded an antique camera. Posed stiffly on the front porch step of a white house, ivy draped on the railing, an unsmiling woman stared potently from the pictures. Was that now Amanda's house? Had this stern woman stood in this very room?

Reflections in silver mirrors undulated. Golden light melted into wallpaper patterns. Photographs implied endlessness. This house had stories to tell. This house held mysteries.

I lifted the lid of an aged ivory box. A collection of tiny black and quartz stones rested on purple velvet. Cradled in a china teacup, a mixture of dried petals radiated illusive spicy scent. An etched crystal bowl offered miniature rose petals and sea shells. Odd treasures, subtle prizes, lay everywhere.

On a low stool by the fireplace, a lone, tattered book caught my eye. Its title tempted me — *Those Who Dare*. Pressed between the yellowed pages, a lavender ribbon marked a page.

"Take a peek." I looked up, startled. There was no one else. Had the room whispered?

The pages fell open to the purple marker. My name, the letters swirled and distinct, was scribbled in the margin followed by three question marks. I slid from curious to nosy, scanning the page, wanting to know why my name was there, what it meant. But Amanda's knock on the door came too soon.

Guilty of snooping, I quickly closed the book, preferring not to be caught. I put the book back on the stool. Intrigued by her time-altering mirrors, her seductive books, her sensuously curved question marks, I hurried to let her in.

Chapter 5

The fire was hot. The game was on. Next to me, on the couch, Amanda's leg lightly pressed against mine. The team? I didn't care. The score? I didn't care. Occasionally, Amanda would grab me as she celebrated the latest touchdown. And I would think, yes, this is good, very good — the warmth of her body, her enticing scent. How could I think of the game, the team, when my body was filled with the most unlikely of sensations?

With a shout, Amanda cheered a call. Her hands rose in the air, then fell. One haphazardly landed on my leg and a jolt of heat seemed to blast from her hand through my body.

Her hand on my thigh, so simple, so intense, evoked vivid memories. That first caress, so many years before, when my girlhood had blossomed into sexual awakening — when tentative fingers on my thigh launched unrivaled sensations through my body.

Amanda's hand innocently resting on my leg reduced me to a touch-hungry adolescent. Heat oozed from her palm, crept slowly up my thigh then pounded in rippling waves between my legs.

"Yes! Yes! Yes!" Amanda shouted. She pulled her hand away and leapt up in the air. "That's it. Superbowl. There's no turning back now!"

A congratulatory hug? I jumped up next to her. She turned to me, as I had hoped, took me in her arms and said, "You'll watch the Superbowl with me, won't you?"

"Yes," I muttered, feeling drugged, euphoric. Being in her arms made me light-headed. How frivolous and distant everything else was in comparison to her, to her touch.

"You know," Amanda said almost in a whisper, "you're very pretty." She ran her finger along my jaw and then into my hair. "A beauty really."

All I could think of was last night when she had kissed me so sweetly on the lips. How I longed for that touch, that particular taste once again!

"Before I kissed you last night," Amanda said softly, the darkness of her eyes deepening, "I wasn't sure if it would be okay with you."

I watched her lips, the color of terra-cotta. They were plush and moist.

"I want you, Veronica." Amanda hesitated. "I know that is all so foreign to you." She gently pushed her hands into my hair. I could feel the pressure of her touch against my scalp.

Was it only one day ago, two, that I couldn't imagine touching a woman? Yet at this moment, it was the only thing I wanted to do, the only thing I had ever wanted to do.

"Amanda —" I could barely hear myself.

"And when we kissed —" Amanda's voice was sweet music — "I could feel that you wanted me. It was in your breath. It was in your heartbeat."

And how right she was. With each inhalation, with each beat of my heart, I wanted her more and more.

"Was I right?" She was a starlit sky. She was a quarter moon. "Do you want me too?"

Yes, I wanted her. But then what? What did that mean? Lying in her arms, stroking her body, running my fingers into her hair, down to her breasts, and what then? Could I actually touch a woman in that sort of way?

"I don't know," I said vaguely. An unexpected anxiety engulfed me. Out of my realm, I was stepping blindly along the edge of a steep cliff.

"And the fact that you're married . . ." Amanda shifted slightly.

Jason! I hadn't even considered him. Amanda and I had kissed. We were talking like lovers. There were more secrets building with each moment. I answered by pulling away from her.

"Perhaps you need to sort this out." Amanda's voice filled with compassion and her midnight eyes became twilight.

Relief swept through me. I wouldn't have to worry about the uncharted territory of making love to a woman. I had a temporary reprieve. There'd be time to consider Jason, time to consider Amanda's touch, there'd be plenty of time.

"Jesus, you missed a great game!" Jason called from the den as I came through the front door.

In no hurry to face him, I hung my raincoat on the coat tree. Amanda consumed me. She was at her cottage yet she was here. All over me, everywhere. I was soaked with her, drenched with the memory of her touch, her scent, her delicate embrace.

In the next room, Jason waited. I was on the edge, on the verge of something unknown. Amanda had kissed me, had tangled her fingers in my hair. My boundaries seemed distorted. Was my friendship with Amanda the beginning of an affair? When I was with her I had an incredible urge to be in her arms. But the reality of caressing her, brushing my lips against her breasts, her belly —

Jason, in his own world, assumed all was well. How could I betray him? I had looked him in the eyes, taken his hands in mine. I had made promises, promises, promises. Yet each moment with Amanda brought more and more secrets.

"So how was your afternoon?" Jason said on his way to the kitchen.

The cream-colored walls contrasted nicely with his mocha complexion. The high-beamed ceilings accented his solid build and strong features. Considering how the house suited him, I had a startling urge to hurry into the rain, to stand in the gray until everything washed away.

"Jason, can we talk a minute?" I forced the words.

Perhaps it was my tone of voice or simply the way my words seemed to slice the air, but Jason stepped from the kitchen into the hall. A sudden seriousness surrounded him.

"Veronica?" His voice held an unfamiliar tension. "You *have* been seeing Amanda, *haven't you*? This hasn't been some sort of a cover for another —"

"Only Amanda," I said, hardly breathing.

"Jeez," Jason interrupted. He shook his head. "Your tone. For a moment, for a brief moment, you had me thinking that there was someone else."

"That's just it, Jason." I took a deep breath. What did I say now? That I was involved, yet I wasn't? That I'd been inadvertently swept into a mysterious passion? That we had kissed but it wasn't sexual? She had touched me but it wasn't physical?

"What are you trying to say?" Jason shifted uneasily.

"I kissed Amanda," I said faintly. I felt like I had unveiled my prized sculpture for an important critic. Standing precariously in a timeless moment, I awaited the telltale approving nod or disappointed frown.

"*Amanda?*" Jason said with an incredulous laugh. "This is about Amanda?"

"Yes," I said, relieved. For it was amusing, wasn't it — all the worrying, all the guilt, over a woman's kiss. "It was quite harmless." I felt giddy, like a small child delighting in a frivolous carousel ride.

"She took me in her arms." I walked over to Jason. "And kissed me like this." I opened my mouth and pressed my lips softly, sweetly, on Jason's — for Amanda's kiss had been so very soft, so very sweet. The light scent of her perfume, the warm velvet of her lips —

The roughness of Jason's beard scratched my face and I impulsively pulled away. Jason stood there, a perplexed look on his face.

"Does that turn you on? Thinking of me kissing a woman?" I asked, no longer in touch with myself. I was out on a tangent, dangling from a limb. A wild exhilaration swept through me. I had stepped outside and come back in.

"I'm not quite sure." Jason seemed bewildered. "Is that why you kissed her? To turn me on?"

"Oh, Jason," I whispered seductively. "Why else?"

Up the stairs, sex with Jason would fix it all. Into bed, sex with Jason would make things clear. In his arms, sex with Jason would set things straight.

"Did you like it?" he whispered as we climbed the stairs.

"Oh, Jason," I giggled. "A woman's kiss? How absurd! What I like is turning you on."

Jason laughed. "I'm a lucky man."

As we fell into bed, a wave of claustrophobia hit me. His cologne was too thick. I felt suffocated, imprisoned. His kiss was too rough, too heavy. We had barely begun, yet I was finished.

"Need to stop," I mumbled. Dizzy and apologizing, I stumbled to the bathroom and locked the door.

* * * * *

When I opened the bathroom door, the room was dark and Jason was snoring. One advantage of football and beer, I thought as I crept downstairs to the kitchen phone.

"Amanda," I lowered my voice as best I could. "It's me, Veronica."

"Veronica!" Amanda's pleasure in hearing my voice was obvious. "What a nice surprise."

"Listen," I continued, still speaking in an undertone. "Can I see you tonight? I need to talk to you."

I glanced at the clock. It was already seven.

"Are you okay? Is something wrong?" Concern was evident in her voice.

"Can I see you tonight?" I repeated. "Is there any way possible?" Did I sound as desperate as I felt? Did Amanda have any idea of the turmoil, the wild tumbling, occurring inside of me? "It's just that —" I searched for words to describe what was actually happening but my mind stumbled across fragments of emotions. There were no exact words.

"Is it Jason?" Amanda said, as if she were attempting to help fill in the blanks.

"No," I muttered. "I mean yes. I mean I don't know what."

"Come to my house," Amanda said quickly. "What time can you get here?"

"Half-hour," I said, relieved that words had come out and that I seemed to be making sense of things.

"I'll be waiting for you."

* * * * *

31

"Sweetheart?"

Startled, I turned. Jason was in the doorway.

"You okay?" He glanced from my eyes to the phone.

Had he heard me? Did he know?

"I don't know what happened . . . upset stomach . . . something I ate . . ." My heart raced. Could he see that I was trembling?

"Sorry," he apologized. "I must have drifted off. Football and beer." He shook his head. "Who was on the phone?"

Did I dare say I had been speaking with Amanda? Would he care? Hadn't he laughed about the frivolous kiss? Hadn't he said it was a sexy fantasy? But if I left now — then how sexy, how frivolous, how absurd would that kiss be?

"Amanda." I tried to sound indifferent. "We're having dinner."

"You're seeing her for dinner? Tonight?" Jason said hesitantly.

"It's nothing, really," I offered, nonchalant.

"Why are you seeing her for dinner? Why tonight?" Jason asked. For some reason his eyes focused on my fingers. Suddenly aware that I had unconsciously been twirling my wedding band, I dropped my hands quickly.

"To tell her —" I paused. To tell her what? "To tell her that we can be friends but the kissing, well, certainly that sort of thing can't go on."

"And this had to take place over dinner?"

"Well, Jason . . ." I smiled, flirtatiously. "You know that's not the kind of thing one says over the phone." It wasn't, was it?

32

Before Jason had a chance to respond, I gave him a quick kiss. "You don't mind, do you?"

"And you'll tell her —"

"Jason." I gave him another kiss. "Of course I will."

I grabbed my coat and hurried into the rain.

When I turned onto the road that led to Amanda's house, I was struck by how quiet and dark it was in the country. A lone yellow light beckoned from her porch. I parked across from her cottage and watched the wooden porch swing rock gently. An eerie shadow swayed on the lawn.

I could envision Amanda as she'd open her door to the warmth of her home. She would enfold me in her arms. She would lead me inside.

I opened the car door, then paused. It was almost as if I knew, somewhere in the heart of me, that once I left the car, there would be no turning back. It was as if Jason, the house, the marriage were all a shimmering dream that faded with each step toward Amanda's door.

Hurry hurry hurry hurry, the night whispered desperately. Scents of evergreen and eucalyptus danced with the raindrops. *Hurry hurry hurry.*

Amanda swung the door open. "Veronica. Are you okay?" She ran through the rain to usher me into her sachet-scented home.

"I don't know what's happening to me." The words poured out. "When I went home this afternoon, I had the most sincere intentions of working things out with Jason. But all I can think of is you."

Helping me with my jacket, Amanda led me to the fireplace where a wood fire crackled. We sat among the large chintz-covered pillows that were tossed in front of the hearth.

"Is that so terribly bad?" Amanda said. She massaged my back gently.

"I just don't understand what I'm feeling." I stared into the flames. Like heated dancers, they swayed and leapt hypnotically. "I'm certainly not a lesbian. I couldn't imagine such a thing. But your touch is —"

Amanda placed her hand under my chin and turned my face toward her. "Veronica, for one simple moment, just stop."

I looked into her eyes where the firelight danced in her deep, coal-colored irises.

"Can you just be here without the worrying? Without the analysis? You like being here, right?" Amanda ran her finger along the side of my face to my ear. "Isn't that all that matters?"

I was momentarily dizzy. The warmth of the fire had grown uncompromisingly hot and I inched back from its abrupt intensity. There was no screen, no barrier from the unpredictable sparks. At any moment, one might leap toward me, set me aflame, burn me. Move back, I thought, unnerved by the erratic fire-dancers. I slid away from the fire into the coolness, craving the calculable safety of the candlelit room.

"Veronica?"

Bathed in delicious coolness from the back of the room, I turned toward Amanda.

"Being here is what you want, isn't it?" She gathered me into her arms, drawing my lips to hers. Her mouth was lush, an oasis. Thirsty, parched by the absolute dryness I felt in the depths of me, I wanted to suck the moisture from the well of her.

Her arms encircled me, enticed me, called me closer to her. Her hands pushed into my hair — a gesture now familiar to me. Pressing her hungry lips against mine, she searched the softness of my mouth with the tip of her tongue.

All I could think of was how good the heat was beginning to feel. I was falling, collapsing, tumbling. Amanda kissed me once, twice, a hundred times, and the flames fanned heat.

I soared to an island. My body pressed against hot sand. Waves slammed the shore.

"Oh yes, oh yes, oh yes," I muttered between tropical kisses — tens, hundreds, thousands of kisses. Sweltering, I untied my string bikini. The hot rays caressed my breasts. "Oh yes, oh yes, oh yes."

Heated hands slid on my skin. Hands, warm with sweat, caressed my breasts. My sun-kissed nipples were burning with desire.

"You are so beautiful. So soft. So fine." Whispered words floated on warm sea breezes.

My neck was damp from the light flicking of Amanda's tongue. Wet heat, sticky heat, encompassed me as though I had never been touched before. Every pore opened in anticipation of soaking in the sweetness of those kisses. Those hot, hot kisses.

In Jason's arms, had it ever been like this? No. Not in Jason's, not in anyone's arms. Not like this. Sultry sensation of lying on a raft, of floating out to sea, drifting with the tide of Amanda's paradise-kisses — it had never been like this.

Her hand slid under my blouse. Heat radiated from her fingertips. Soft on my belly, hot on my belly, her determined touch was light. My nipples hardened under my bra and pushed angrily against the silk.

Amanda kissed my breasts through my blouse and my nipples strained desperately for attention. Hard like pellets, hard like pink quartz — more more more.

Her hand slid into my pants. I knew what she'd find. Wet and creamy, thick and sticky — more more more.

"Is this what you want? Is this okay?"

More. More. More, my body cried. *Yes.* My body ached. "I don't know. I don't know."

"Do you want me to stop?" Amanda's voice was distinct. She pulled away. Her lips were no longer mine. I opened my eyes to be greeted by the sputtering fire and the cool room.

How long had we lay in front of the fire kissing? Seeming like mere seconds, it was not nearly enough. Yet, it was forever. We had been kissing for eternity.

Amanda held me in her arms and I clung to her. Like a child in rough waters, I feared being swept away if I let go. Why had she stopped? Why had I let her?

My body ached as though I had been slammed against the floor. I felt as if I'd been suspended in the eye of a delicious hurricane. Not thinking, not questioning how I felt or what it meant, I had been enfolded in warm currents of wind. All had been magically calm until her words: *Is this okay?*

But it wasn't okay. I was married. It wasn't quite right; she was a woman.

"Yes, yes, too much," I stuttered. I struggled to gain my composure.

Amanda tossed a log into the withering fire. Within seconds the rejuvenated flames hungrily surged to devour the fresh wood.

"I'm sorry," she said softly. "I didn't want to push you if you weren't ready."

Yes, I thought, confused. We had moved too quickly. There were things to consider. Important consequences to contemplate. Caught up, led astray by a warm fire, a bewitching moment, I was out of control.

"I should go," I said uneasily. I stared at the flame-shrouded wood. I was not ready to look into Amanda's captivating eyes.

"Veronica," Amanda whispered, her lips teasing my ear. I felt the heat of her breath as she spoke. "I'll be here for you. Tonight, tomorrow, you just say the word and I'm here." She walked to the bookcase and returned with a small, knotted, tapestry pouch. "For you, for sweet dreams. Put this under your pillow tonight."

I gently kneaded the woven bag between my fingers. An unexpected wisp of mingled scents — peppermint, cloves, orange blossoms and anise — filled the air.

"Thank you for tonight," I said half-heartedly.

A battle raged within. I wanted to push her

away. I wanted to grab onto her. I wanted to run away yet stay forever. It wasn't Amanda but it was. It wasn't her kisses but it was.

"You will come back?" Amanda followed me to the door. The tone of her words implied fact.

"Yes." I glanced past her to the radiant hearth. The flames called to me. I could stay. I could sprinkle the contents of the pouch into the flames. Imagining the colors, the tiny sparks, as the herbs spilled, I stared at the fire.

Amanda put her arms around me and kissed my neck. She then muttered something under her breath, and if I hadn't seen those very words in her book, I would have never been able to decipher what she had said.

"I'm sorry?" I turned from the fire to her eyes. I wanted her to repeat the words and expand on their meaning.

"Just call me," Amanda said. She gave me one last hug. "Call me soon."

I stayed in her arms for a brief moment then hurried to my car. Amanda waved and the front door closed.

The air was crisp. The dark night was silent. I stared at her small house. My eyes were drawn to the dim light that barely escaped from the curtained window. A dog's quick bark broke the calm and then the night became still.

I didn't want to leave. Reluctance at the idea of going home to Jason was overwhelming. I walked back to the porch. On impulse, I tiptoed to the window and peeked into the small split between the curtains. Amanda, in front of the fire, was bent over, working on something.

I considered knocking. I knew she'd let me stay. If only Jason and that other world would disappear, I'd be free. But free to go where? Confusion returned.

Jason waited. Home waited. Whatever was here would have to wait, too.

Carefully squeezing the tapestry bag, I inhaled its seductive fragrance. The mystery of Amanda's elusive words seemed woven with the exotic scent.

Those who dare.

Those who dare.

Those who dare.

Chapter 6

Book in hand, Jason was sprawled on the couch when I came in. Not in the mood for conversation, I offered a quick hello and headed for the stairs. The tub, filled to the brim with hot bubbles, was my destination. The heated, steamy bathroom was the only place I wanted to be.

"Hey! Not so fast," Jason called after me. "How'd it go?"

I leaned back into the den. "Okay."

Hoping not to be drawn in further, I averted my eyes from Jason to the painting that hung above the couch. Although the picture had occupied that spot since we moved in, this was the first time I had studied it carefully.

It was a simple portrait of two horses shadowed in black and brown hues. Yet tonight, their faces, silhouetted by jagged manes, caught my attention. With flared nostrils and an unsettling erratic fury in their eyes, the horses appeared to be staring specifically at me. Was it my imagination or was the wooden picture frame actually bulging, barely able to contain the horses? In their unbridled power, the horses seemed ready to burst from their insubstantial confines.

"So how'd she take it? Did you break her heart?"

"Break her heart?" I repeated. I forced my gaze from the painting to the cocky expression on Jason's face. He had suddenly gotten on my nerves.

"You know, the kiss," he smirked. "It's quite amusing, wouldn't you say? A lesbian coming on to you, thinking that perhaps . . ." He chuckled. "I mean you, of all women!"

"What's that supposed to mean?" I said defensively. "What's so amusing about a woman finding me attractive?"

"Veronica." Jason glanced over the top of his book. "No cause for alarm. I didn't mean that you're not attractive. Heavens no! What's amusing is that you're so into men. Of all the women for her to take a liking to!"

I turned back toward the stairs. His ability to deny things relieved and irritated me simultaneously. I wanted nothing more of this conversation, nothing more of Jason.

"So?" he yelled after me.

"So it went fine," I called down to him. "Just fine."

I suppose that had been enough, for Jason neither called me nor followed me up the stairs.

"Good," I mumbled to the tub, as if we were co-conspirators in avoiding Jason.

The bath was my luxury, my own paradise. I created sensual moods with simple acts. Three candles were lit so that a golden canopy tented the navy-tiled tub. Lavender-scented oils were dribbled into the flowing water. Doors were closed to capture the steam.

As round hills of bubbles grew in the tub, I slowly removed my clothes. In the steam-filled, dimly lit, secluded room, my reflection in candlelight looked seductively erotic. Unhooked, my silk bra fell to the floor. The warm dampness kissed my breasts and my nipples swelled.

In the mirror, I saw Amanda. Her hot-honey kisses, I could taste on my lips. Her strong hands, I could feel on my back. Her sizzling words, I could hear them still. She was the steam in the air. She was the perspiration on my breasts. She was the heated water, the cool tile, the smooth soap, the thick bubbles.

The hot water stung as I eased in. The vision of Amanda, surrounded by pillows of bubbles, was waiting for me. Her dark hair pinned up, her pale skin like ivory — she wore nothing but pink lipstick and a textured kitchen glove.

"Oh, Amanda," I murmured as I lifted my legs to the sides of the tub.

She soaped me, lathered my feet, my calves, my thighs. The glove, covered with small raised latex knobs, invigorated my flesh as she massaged.

"Feel good?" she asked.

I spread my legs further. There was so much more that needed a good scrub.

The nubbed fingers kneaded my inner thighs. I sank deeper, raised my legs higher. Down into the tub, down in the heat, water engulfed my shoulders, my neck. Light feather touches tickled and teased.

I whimpered.

She covered my eyes with a heated washcloth. She poured cool water down my face.

The fingers, covered with rugged protrusions, separated my pussy and nuzzled the folds. One on each side, the bumpy fingertips slid up and down the length of my clitoral shaft. She stroked me over and over, up and down, those knotty fingers squeezed and pulsed.

I turned on the faucet. Hot, as hot as I could take it, the water rushed into the tub. Streaming water hit directly on my pleasure, lapping and pressing with a delicious force. And Amanda, sweet Amanda, continued to flatten my clit.

The water whipped my pussy, vibrated my pussy. Hips out of the water. How far could I get? Could I push my pussy against the faucet? Then how close? How hard could the water push me? How fast?

Oh, Amanda. So good, Amanda. The water was hot. The water was fast. The water was so good.

Her fingers grabbed the rim of my slit, then

pulled it open and stretched it tight. The water pounded, the water pumped — first the opening of my cunt, then the clit. Back to the opening, then the clit, the water surged relentlessly.

The water was strong. The water was ongoing. My clit was fire and the water spilled. The water pressed. The water blasted.

Amanda, please don't stop.

Amanda's ribbed fingers dipped into the entrance. She rubbed, she kneaded, she stroked the inner flesh.

How high could I push up? How hard could the water beat? Legs spread, all right. Hips raised, all right. Amanda's fingers, like swirling beaters, prodded and probed as the water slammed hard.

Relaxed, released, I soaked in the fantasy of Amanda.

The door opened, cool air flooded the bathroom and Amanda disappeared with the steam.

"Room for one more in that bath?" Jason began unbuttoning his shirt.

"I was just getting out." Grabbing a towel, I hurriedly wrapped it around myself as though instinctively covering my nakedness.

"Going to sleep then?" He followed me to the bed and sat next to me.

"Yeah, long day," I said, feigning a yawn.

"What with all the running around, huh?" Jason tried to kiss me but I turned from him, pretending to check the clock. Jason's mouth certainly did not belong where Amanda's honey nectar still glazed my lips.

"What is it?" Jason said intently. "You seem distant."

"Tired, that's all." I closed my eyes.

"Tired? That's all it is?" Jason clicked off the light.

"Very tired," I answered softly. I reached to the nightstand and placed the small scented pouch under my pillow. Very tired indeed.

It was nine-thirty. Sunday morning ritual had Jason gone by nine for croissants and the paper. As soon as I heard the door close, I called Amanda.

"Did you dream?"

Amanda's first words caught me off guard. Oddly enough — because I was not one to dream, or remember if I had — last night I had had an incredibly vivid dream.

"Well, yes," I said, surprised by her question.

"Tell me," Amanda urged.

I ran my finger along the dark green comforter, considering the dream. "Let's see . . . I was walking down this path and the air smelled sweet — orange blossoms or something like that. I heard a galloping horse so I ran down the path to a field. I remember hundreds of little flowers everywhere. A large black horse broke into the clearing. Suddenly, he became a lioness. Her teeth were bared and her eyes filled with fierceness. I was frightened for my life but I couldn't move. I covered my eyes and fell to my knees. Everything was dark. I waited for the attack but there was nothing. It was quiet. So I peeked between my fingers and a beautiful white mare stood before me. A scroll of paper in a braided leather band hung from her neck. I took it and read it. *The visitor might learn the secrets.* The horse took several steps away from me and spread her great white wings and whispered, 'Passage?' Then I woke up."

"A winged horse?" Amanda seemed excited.

The front door closed. Jason had returned and was heading upstairs.

"Amanda, I've got to go. Can I see you today?" I asked quickly.

"Yes, please!" She seemed as anxious as I. "Early afternoon?"

Jason was in the hall.

"Around one," I whispered and hung up.

Jason tossed the paper on the bed. "Who was that?" he asked. But we both knew the answer. What followed was the first fight Jason and I had had in a while.

"Why are you seeing Amanda again today?" he demanded.

And what could I say? That I liked spending time with Amanda more than I did with him? Which was the absolute truth, but there was no way I could tell him that.

But as it happened, I didn't have to say a word. Before I could think of a plausible explanation, Jason was already one step ahead of me.

"You spent yesterday with her. Let's you and I spend the day together."

An out-of-character statement for Jason, whose Sundays were booked well in advance. If not TV sports, there was always his precious antique car that needed work.

"Since when do you have time on Sunday?" I walked over to the dressing table.

"Since you started playing footsie with some diesel dyke." Jason's voice had lowered into an unnatural monotone.

"Excuse me?" I reacted instantly. "Is that what she is now, *some diesel dyke?*"

"Well, what would you have me call her? Huh? Seems to me you and your dyke buddy are getting pretty damn chummy. No time for me, cold as ice toward me." Jason started pacing. "What's the story, Veronica? Is she turning you into one of them? Is that the next thing you're going to come home and tell me? That you like women? Or are you going to just let me find the two of you in bed."

And there it was. Perhaps it was the statement I'd wished for all along. I finally had a good reason to stomp around the room, grab my clothes and storm out of the house.

"Yes!" I shouted. I threw a pillow at him. "One of them! She's turning me into one of them! And I couldn't be happier!"

"Oh that's just great," Jason called after me. "Just fucking great."

I grabbed my jeans, a sweater, and headed down the stairs.

I swerved onto Amanda's road. Turning off the ignition, I took a moment to think. Without even considering, I had jumped in the car and headed straight for Amanda's. I glanced at my watch, it was ten. I was several hours early. Was I being presumptuous, showing up at her house unannounced? Perhaps she would perceive this as an intrusion of her space, her privacy. I was about to turn around when the front door opened.

"I thought I heard a car," Amanda called from the porch. Her voice unraveled like a spring bouquet tossed in the air.

"I hope it's okay that I just showed up." I walked toward the porch. The storm had cleared and the sky was blue. "Jason and I had a fight and I —"

"Of course it's okay." Amanda took my hand and led me into her house.

Except for a small desk lamp that had been placed on the floor by the fireplace, the living room was dark. Amanda had not yet drawn the curtains. Spread out near the lamp were woven pouches, like the one Amanda had given me. A tattered book lay in the center.

"Sit down. I'll get us some tea. We can talk." Amanda pulled back the curtains and disappeared into the kitchen.

Light streamed into the room and spotlighted the book. On impulse, I stepped closer. *Those Who Dare* — the title, chipped gold Celtic letters. The purple ribbon sliced between the yellowed pages.

Amanda, still in the kitchen, hummed. I flipped the book open — nosy or not, now was my chance — but what I saw was not my name. Instead a white-winged horse stared at me from the page. The word *passage* was scribbled beneath it.

"Amanda?" An eerie chill ricocheted through me. "Amanda?"

Wordlessly, Amanda placed the tea tray on the coffee table.

"This is the exact horse that was in my dream." I gazed at Amanda who had not moved. Her eyes appeared momentarily vacant and she seemed lost in thought.

"Amanda?"

As if suddenly ignited, she hurried to my side. "Veronica, you can't imagine —" She rushed the words, her voice barely more than a whisper. "There is so much to tell you. I didn't think now was the time . . . You were so upset when you came in and I didn't want to —" She reached for the book and knelt next to me. "When you told me your dream this morning, I could hardly believe it. It worked — the dream bags, the herbs — I brought this horse to your dreams. With the dream bag, the proper meditations —" She closed her eyes for a brief instant. Her hands trembled as though a slight current raced through her. "And you!" Her electric-black eyes abruptly opened. "I had hoped, I'd fantasized that I could take you with me into a dream. But I had no idea it would be so easy."

I couldn't speak, didn't know what to say.

Amanda pointed to the white horse and read the caption beneath the picture. *"The winged horse carries the seeker to the dream world.* Last night I chanted. I envisioned the horse offering you transport." She dropped the book to the floor and grasped me tightly. "You have dreamed the dream.

The horse, the field, all of it orchestrated right here with this book and these herbs!"

She began kissing me over and over. "Veronica, come with me on a dream journey!"

Her warm hands interlocked with mine. She kissed my lips, my eyes, my cheeks. Lightly, she nipped my chin then my neck. Gently licking, her hot tongue flicked warmth across my shoulder. She grasped my hands tighter.

"Say yes, Veronica. Please, Veronica." Her words were muffled, less distinct.

She sucked my tender skin into her mouth and a hot current surged from her to me. Every nerve ending buzzed frantically. Trembling waves rose.

My nipples tightened as if a live wire were stimulating them unmercifully. Her knowing mouth moved closer. As if we had always been lovers, as if it had always been this way, I unbuttoned my shirt for her.

Beet-red, my nipples were desperately hard. And she knew, oh she knew. Teasing the areolas, she flicked with her warm tongue. The smooth pink contracted into rouge-waved flesh. My nipples ached. I forced her mouth to me and begged her to suck.

"Please, Amanda. Please." As if we had always been lovers, as if it had always been this way, I pleaded.

I pressed my body to hers. She pressed hers to mine. The pressure of her hipbone against my mound was direct. Rocking, grinding, she rode me. I grabbed her, moved with her. We were wild with passion. I cried out as I slammed against her strong hip.

Amanda pinched my nipple between her teeth —

almost too hard, not hard enough. I moaned. Amanda panted. Her mouth still sucked. Her hands pushed into my pants.

Her skillful fingers wasted no time sliding into my secret juices. They churned across my tingling clit. Easy circles, soft circles, they teased me to a swollen bud. Not stopping, she increased suction on my nipple. Not stopping, she rubbed.

I tightened my thighs and ass, creating a sweet tension. My legs stiff, I liked it. My ass hard, I liked it. With repeated, concentrated contractions, I fluttered my vaginal muscles. I tightened, then released, again and again.

As Amanda's fingers beat faster, my pussy opened and closed. Her rhythm was unremitting and I kept in time. Ongoing, she strummed. Ongoing, I pinched and opened. The intensity climbed. The tension hardened. One finger felt like two, felt like three, felt like four. Thick, fast, hard, constant — Amanda kept on.

"Relax," she whispered but I kept myself taut. I knew what I needed. I knew how it went. Tighter and tighter, I pressed up to her hand.

Lost in the throbbing, my passion unfolded. Thick-syrup pleasure mounted. Tension expanded then burst into ecstasy. Currents shot through me like never before. Every muscle contracted into rapturous knots. And I rode it out. Like riding a wild stallion, I bucked and flailed until release brought me home.

Moments in after-passion drift fast yet drag slow.

I struggled to open my eyes but could not see. Amanda was on top of me, her breathing deep, steady.

You. I heard whispering, although Amanda hadn't stirred.

We'll ride to a forest where rainbows burst from cascading waterfalls. To mountaintops where snow is spun from beaded crystals. Where pastel scents drizzle from perfume clouds.

"Amanda?" I whispered. Amanda was still, as though sleeping.

Mingled scents of anise and jasmine, peppermint and clove came from the darkness. Faintly, I heard the gallop of an approaching horse but it was muffled in the wail of wild winds that had suddenly taken us.

Amanda:
The Dream Journeys

Chapter 7

When Veronica went with me on that first dream
journey, it was completely unexpected. I had never
fallen into a dream without extensive preparation.
Yet without the dream bags and without the
meditations, Veronica and I had been swept into a
dream-storm.

It came from nowhere, lasted only seconds, then
abruptly ended. As if whirling in an untamed
hurricane, winds seemed to surround us. We spun,
hanging onto each other, until the dream fragment
subsided.

Veronica — everything about her was unexpected. Women in relationships and straight women — I made a habit to avoid them both. Even so, I was obsessed with her. She filled my thoughts constantly. Everywhere my imagination wandered, I found her waiting.

When I met Veronica, my dreams shifted to clouded figments filled with fragmented images of her. In dream-shadows her lips whispered my name, her alluring eyes pleaded with me. Drawn to her, forced by something deep within, I made my move.

I gave her a dream bag, I don't know why. It seemed appropriate. It seemed right. It seemed out of my hands. Chanting and meditating, oblivious to consequences, I called her into my dreams.

When Veronica told me she dreamed about the winged horse, I was shocked. Torn between telling her everything and slowly educating her, I tried to set boundaries. But when she showed up at my house and found the book, I fell off course. Caught up in excitement, I found my plan of gradual disclosure unraveling rapidly.

I brought her into my arms thinking that this was meant to be. Words began to pour from me. She was in my arms and I kissed her as if we had always kissed. Words melted into overflowing passion. Spilling from me, my desire flooded us both. My mouth and fingers sought her. I caressed her. I cascaded into her. This was meant to be.

Voices, in waves of whispers, surrounded me. *Take her with you. Take her now.* One moment I was in her arms, the next in a windstorm. The winds passed in a matter of seconds but I was shaken. The journeys had never been like that before, so haphazard, so out of control. There was no question that I'd have to be more careful, bearing in mind the energy that Veronica and I seemed to evoke.

But Veronica was like a changed person.

"Did you feel that?" she said excitedly. "Did you hear the winds, feel the rumbling?"

Not frightened, she seemed less out of sorts than I.

"Amanda, was that it? Is that how it works? Let's do it again. Let's go into a dream right now!" She grabbed my hands. "What must we do to go further? Lie down? Take a nap together?"

A dream journey with her, so soon? I lacked experience but what harm could come of it? The few times I'd taken the night journeys were like brief romps in a Hollywood dream clip. What difference would Veronica's company make? Isn't this what I had wanted? Things were moving faster than I'd planned, that's all. The dream world beckoned.

Veronica grasped my hands and looked at me with fervent hope. She begged me to take her into the dreams, right that instant. She had a look in her eyes that made refusal impossible.

I led her to my bedroom and sprinkled the contents of a dream bag across the bed. The room filled with the familiar scent of dream travel. I lit three white candles that graced the altar at the head of my bed. I lifted the small sculpture of Diana, my bronze goddess, given to me years before. I stroked her carefully before returning her to her platform.

I sat on the edge of the bed and motioned for Veronica to come to me. She ran her fingers through her cherry-brown hair. Her dark eyes, with their suggestion of Oriental ancestry, sparkled with excitement.

This is it, I thought rapturously. After we had explored the dream world together, Veronica and I would be irrevocably bonded.

"Lie in my arms," I said softly.

She lay in my arms. I felt her slight trembling.

"Sweet dreams," I murmured and began to chant.

We are walking down a path and Veronica is holding my hand. We are in a forest, enclosed by tall trees. It is afternoon but the sun's light is filtered by the thickness of the foliage.

Veronica turns to me and is suddenly surrounded by shimmering colors. Watermelon pinks, bright greens, sapphire blues. She starts to speak but the words turn into musical notes. I watch them float from her pink lips.

"I want you."

I take her into my arms. The warm summer breeze fans her hair.

"Yes, Amanda." The notes swirl around her. "I want you too."

The trees are gone. We are in a field and the sun is hot. Veronica walks toward me. She has removed her top. The pink of her nipples matches the pink of her lips.

I step toward her. I long to touch the softness of her breasts. I am impatient to taste her lips on mine. My shirt falls to the ground, my pants fall to my knees. I am surprised, but very pleased, to see a large, latticed dildo strapped around my hips. It is a smooth, soft peach-colored latex. I have seen pictures of this kind of sex toy and can imagine the pleasure its bulky, crossed strips would bring.

Only inches from me, Veronica touches the dildo tentatively. She has a smile on her face and a twinkle in her eyes. Her nipples are flat against her wide areolas. I run my fingertips down her shoulders to the curve of her full breasts and her nipples stiffen to hardened points. There is nothing like her smooth skin. Nothing rivals the firmness of her rose-budded breasts.

I press my tongue against her. Her neck tastes salty from the heat. I reach under her short skirt. My fingers dip into her sweet well. Moist and slick, her hidden folds are thick. Her tiny bead eludes me.

I separate her creased, full flesh and guide the dildo tip to her slit. Veronica moans as I hit a tender place. I hold her waist and lift her. She is weightless and floats directly above my extended latticework. I keep her in place and slowly lower her onto the ribbed thickness.

I raise her until her lips dangle on the bulbous tip. She is so light, I can elevate and sink her with one hand. Her skirt is hiked to her waist and her pussy is dark red. As she glides up and down, as I move her in slow motion, I watch the dildo spear into her. Her opalescent cream smears as she moves and her labia grab and stick.

I like this dream. I like the freedom to please Veronica in innovative ways — ways not possible awake — like leaning her back. Like watching her fat pussy swallow my toy.

I pull out of her, turn her around and press the

toy against her ass. I push, I burrow back into her slit, moving Veronica side to side. I turn her nice and slow. I watch as her entrance clamps the latticed trespasser. She is upside down. Her skirt has flipped up and she's completely exposed. I fuck her like this. I turn her again. Her slit sucks the bumpy dildo as she rotates. I fuck her like that. I turn her. I glide her up and down with ease.

I can play with her breasts. I can friction-rub her clit. I can pump her and turn her anyway I can imagine.

A thunderous galloping sound jars my attention. I quickly pull Veronica off the dildo. An ominous cloud covers the sun. The sky darkens. In the near distance, racing against the lightness of the sun, comes a horsewoman dressed in black.

Toward me, toward Veronica, she rides a midnight stallion. The air fills with a sudden scent, an unpredictable scent, a most disarming scent of hot peppers and spice. The horsewoman is upon us. She passes behind Veronica and in that brief moment, she swoops down, diving like a hawk or a vulture — and lifts my Veronica, carries my Veronica into the forest.

I stand there, stunned and alone. The cloud slips from the sun and a demanding heat overpowers the field. I am unbearably hot, I fear fainting and cannot take a simple step.

Immobilized, I can only stare at the wooded path where Veronica has disappeared. And into the quiet emptiness, I begin to scream, "Veronica!"

* * * * *

"Veronica! Veronica!"

Covered in a profuse sweat, I jerked out of my dream. Veronica was next to me seemingly lost in a deep sleep.

"What a dream," I said, although Veronica did not stir.

Embracing Veronica, I listened to the hypnotic rhythm of her breath. I considered waking her but her body was so relaxed, her peaceful breathing so mesmerizing.

The sound was melodic. The inhalation was spellbinding, the exhalation entrancing. I should wake her, I thought vaguely. An overwhelming desire to close my eyes, to rest just a bit more, swept through me.

Her breathing was slow.

Perhaps just for a moment, I'd close my eyes.

Her breathing was deep.

Just a moment, then I'd wake her.

Her breathing was calming . . .

Struggling as I cut through thick bushes, I hack the branches with a machete. I can only guess in what direction Veronica has gone.

The sun is setting. It doesn't matter. There is nothing else until I find her, until I bring her back.

I hear the ringing of a bell. Carving my passage through the brush, the ringing is persistent.

* * * * *

I looked at the clock. One-thirty. The telephone was ringing insistently. Groggy from the dream, I grabbed the receiver.

"Amanda? This is Karen."

"Karen." I sat up in hopes of shaking the fog. How odd to have slept so soundly in midday.

"Listen," Karen said quickly. "Veronica's husband just called me. He wanted your number. He was looking for Veronica." She paused as though waiting for my reaction but continued before I had a chance. "I don't know what's going down but he sounded really upset. I'm supposed to call him back."

At that moment I realized Veronica was no longer in my bed.

"Veronica?" I called out toward the living room. There was no answer. "Karen, hold just a minute."

I tossed the receiver aside and climbed out of bed. My head began to throb.

"Veronica?"

The living room was empty. The house was quiet. I hurried to the window. Veronica's car was still parked on the road.

"Her car's here," I mumbled to Karen. "I guess she went for a walk." I massaged my pounding temple. "She mentioned they had had a fight."

"Well, he wants to talk to her," Karen said sternly. "What's going on, Amanda? There's nothing between you and Veronica is there? Is there?" Karen sounded exasperated. "Should I give him your number?"

"Tell him she'll call him when she gets in," I said, distracted.

"Yeah, well, I'll try," Karen said reluctantly. "But what's the story?"

"Later, Karen."

I was spinning. The throbbing was unbearable. I hung up, then took the phone off the hook. Perhaps I was coming down with the flu. Needing just a moment to escape the pulsating pressure, I closed my eyes, needing a moment to escape. My lids were heavy and the pain continued.

I stand in front of a lake. The reflection of the full-orbed moon lights up the entire valley. In the far distance I hear the crying of wolves. The jagged mountains, from which the howling descends, provide a purple backdrop.

I am tired. I have searched all day. I have traveled only on instinct, not knowing, not certain, where they have gone. Yet, I sense that I'm on their trail and that I haven't lost them entirely.

I worry about Veronica. She wore no shirt when she was carried into the woods. The night air is chilly. What will she do for warmth?

There is a rustling in the brush. A raccoon steals toward an old log.

"You!" I call out.

The raccoon stops. The reflection of the moon glimmers in his eyes.

The raccoon does not speak but I can hear his thoughts.

"The wolves, always the wolves." He scurries away into the darkness.

I don't think I can wander any more tonight but I'm too frightened to close my eyes. I'm afraid to sleep in these woods.

* * * * *

I opened my eyes to the darkened bedroom. The insistent glow from the clock caught my attention. Seven-thirty. I had slept the entire day.

I turned on the lamp. Veronica was not in bed. "Veronica?" The house was uncomfortably quiet. Perhaps she had left for home.

Hurrying to the front window, I was uncertain if I felt relief or alarm when I saw her car still parked in the darkness. I opened the front door and yelled into the night.

"Veronica?"

There was a distant barking of dogs but nothing more. An image of howling wolves flashed through me followed by a profound uneasiness. I turned back into the house. The dream book still lay on the living room floor. On instinct, I opened to the purple ribbon between the yellowed pages.

I felt dizzy, disoriented, needing to sit. Staring out from the page, trapped in a black and white image, was a large dark wolf. In my handwriting, three words were scribbled beneath it. *Always the wolves.*

Veronica:
The Dream World

Chapter 8

I stared into the fire. As the flames licked the wood, the rich scent of eucalyptus and pine inundated me. I thought back to the last fire I had gazed into. A vague image of Amanda wavered, dream-like.

The horsewoman was building a fire. Night had fallen and the dark surrounded us like deep-curtained velvet. She smiled and the orange glow from the fire burned like inextinguishable embers in her black eyes. Her jet hair was bound tightly in a braid that hung halfway down her back. Tight black leggings emphasized her lean, muscular build.

Studying her face, I pondered her lineage. Her thin lips, a deep pink, were emphasized by her rich, sable coloring. Strong cheekbones yielded to a sculptured Romanesque nose. And her dark-lashed eyelids, shadowed in grays and lined with charcoal, brought to mind Cleopatra.

"You are awake?" Her Egyptian eyes locked into mine.

Had I been asleep? Sporadic fragments of the day flooded me. I remembered being swept into a black-clouded hurricane. There was a hypnotic beat of hoofs and then Amanda and the field had disappeared.

As she stoked the fire, I tried to pull myself from the ground but felt dazed, as if waking from a drug-laden fog. Fleeting hallucinations swirled around me: I envisioned Amanda, alone in the field. A beaming sun poured liquid heat from the sky and she was calling for me. A rainbow began drizzling colored flakes and the image of Amanda faded.

"You have come home, Feronia. You have come back to me." The horsewoman spoke distinctly, as if each word were carefully chiseled.

Her words were clear but the colored flakes were thick and response was difficult.

"Feronia?" the woman said, glancing at me as she placed another log on the fire.

I propped myself on my elbows, a bed of thick furs beneath me. Mountain walls loomed above us under a star-dotted sky. Had time passed slowly or quickly? I was disoriented and uncertain.

"Who are you?" My mouth was dry and the words came hard.

"So you have forgotten." The woman's statement was definitive.

"This is just a dream," I said faintly.

"And the memory of our love escapes you?"

Our love? A sudden dark design drifted across the face of the full moon and the night air seemed to cool momentarily. Yes, this was an extraordinary dream.

I looked deep into her kohl-rimmed eyes. "This is a dream," I repeated. "I have no memory of you."

The woman brushed her soft lips against my ear.

"Then you have not yet woken," she growled and sharply bit my tender lobe.

The tone in her voice — deep and intimate . . . Suddenly I remembered. Her wild-animal scent, alluring, intoxicatingly familiar . . . Yes, I remembered. Her gleaming teeth, razor-sharp against my skin . . . Dear goddess, I remembered!

The bite caused me to cry out. I jerked forward. I was in a field. The outline of Amanda's home stood distinctly against the fullness of the moon.

"Devana!" I screamed into the night but there was no answer.

* * * * *

"Amanda! Amanda!" I banged on her cottage door. I wasn't sure how long I had been outside but I was trembling.

The front door opened immediately.

"Thank God!" Amanda pulled me into the warmth. "Where have you been? Your car was here but I couldn't find you."

"I guess I —"

"And Jason!" Her voice had a frantic edge. "Karen gave him my number. He's called three times already. Out for a walk, I told him. 'Out for a walk in the night?' he says. 'Veronica *doesn't* take walks in the night alone.' And what could I say? I've been worried sick." Amanda embraced me. Her body radiated a delicious heat. "It's just that I care for you. I care so much for you, Veronica."

I pulled back slightly and peered into Amanda's onyx eyes.

"The dream, Amanda," I said, exhilarated. I didn't care about Jason. I didn't care about the worries. It was the dream and Devana that called for me now. "I had this extraordinary dream. We need to lie down. We need to go back."

"Well, yes, of course, we can experiment." Amanda shifted, her voice became vague. "There will be plenty of opportunities . . . after I study a few more techniques, gain a bit more control."

"More control?" I said wildly. "Who needs control? It was wonderful, exciting, like wandering through a movie. Like nothing I've experienced before. Didn't you dream? Wasn't it that way for you?"

The sharp ring of the telephone caused Amanda

to turn away. "It's him, you know." Her face tightened.

"I don't want to talk," I said in an abrupt tone. "Say I went for coffee. Tell him anything."

Not moving, Amanda stared at the phone. It rang one last time then stopped.

"Good." I wove Amanda's hand into mine and led her to the couch. "Didn't you dream?" I said again, not bothering to wait for her reply. "My dream was incredible. I was with you in this field and then you were gone. Is that how it works? We have separate journeys?"

"Did you dream of the horsewoman?" Amanda asked, her tone serious.

"My God!" I was stunned. "Yes! Devana! You dreamt of her, too?"

"The horsewoman stole you. From out of nowhere she tore you away from me. I spent the entire day searching for you. It was like being lost in a nightmare."

"No, Amanda, it wasn't a nightmare at all!" Excitement buzzed through me. "We got separated, that's all. It was an adventure. Let's go back. We can go together this time."

"That's just it, Veronica," Amanda said. As if avoiding me, she tugged distractedly at a loose thread on her pants. "I'm worried that I'll lose you again. I lost control. That's never happened to me before. I'm not quite sure what this means or what could happen. Do you even remember leaving the bed? Do you remember going outside?"

I took a moment to digest her words. She had a point. I had no memory of my activity.

"I'll review the techniques, study the elements," Amanda said, her voice calm. She motioned to the dream book. "It only makes sense to be able to pilot a plane before take-off."

I nodded in disappointed agreement.

She gave me a quick kiss on the cheek and then reached for the book. "I suppose I did some sleepwalking myself. Look what I wrote in my sleep." She pointed to a page.

It wasn't her handwritten words that caught my attention. It was the image in the photograph. A lone dark wolf stared from the picture. The eyes were focused directly into mine. Riveted, I could not turn away. Instead, with absolutely no reasonable explanation, I began to sob.

I cried, filled with a deep longing but for what, I was unsure. Amanda laid the book on the floor and took me in her arms.

"Dear Veronica," she said softly. She ran her hands through my hair. "This has been exhausting, hasn't it?"

"Yes," I muttered. I was completely out of sorts. "All of a sudden, I feel so alone. I have no idea what's happening inside of me."

Amanda pressed her thick, warm lips against my ear.

"You've been through a lot today," she murmured. "The fight with Jason, the dream, sleepwalking — you must be overwhelmed. Believe me, Veronica, it may seem difficult, but you're *not* alone. I'm here. Let me fill the loneliness." She began kissing me, small kisses, tender kisses, on my lips, my tear-stained cheeks, my ears. "I'll care for you. I'll take care of you."

Amanda unbuttoned my blouse. Her hands felt strong against my skin. I liked them there, wanted them there. I arched my back slightly, encouraging them to move to my breasts.

Tingling, my nipples began to throb. I was desperate for her fingers to brush, then roughly push along the curve of my breasts. I wanted her to work my nipple, grab my nipple, twist, pull, suck my nipple. From soft pink tips to hard, red points. I knew she could take me there.

Her hands slid across the slope of my breast. Inches, only inches from the tightened flushed skin, her fingers teased. My areolas, thirsting for touch, gathered into claret-red ripples.

Her fingertip flicked lightly above my nipple. Out of control, I moaned. I was impassioned, swept into fear. Impatient for her fingers to make their landing, my nipples stood like raspberry-tinted arrow tips. I grabbed her hand and pushed it against my nipple. I wanted her fingers pulling on the thick, puckered stubs.

"Please, oh yes," I cried as she finally plucked the skin between her fingers.

She snapped my nipple, tweaked it. My entire body ached with desire.

Amanda sucked the pleated skin into her mouth. Her lush, wet lips nursed hungrily. She stretched then released my nipple. Tugged then liberated. Each time the suction broke, there was a sensuous clicking sound. My nipple, enlarged as never before, was tinted in a raw red.

I burned for more. I wanted her fingers everywhere — on my belly, in my panties, between my lips, deep in my slit.

Amanda was right with me, as if she read my every thought. *Yes, I'll touch you there. Like that? You want the nipple pinched? You want your panties down? I'll take your panties down.*

Right with me, all the way — she started to remove my panties. I grabbed at them, pulled at them, would help in any way. Down, away, I needed them off now.

They were soaked. A pearly film, moist and sticky, shimmered on the thin material like white frosting. Amanda brought the panties to her mouth. She licked the sugary glaze and moaned.

"Oh, baby. Spread your legs for me," Amanda said, her voice suddenly deeper.

Anything, anything she would have asked in that moment, I would have done. I spread my legs. I was panting.

Her fingers moved to my soft entrance. She dipped them. She swirled them lightly in my dampness, then spread her fingers. My fluid, like glimmering white spider-silk, was strung between them.

She slipped her fingers back to my mound. One finger rested against my sex.

"Your sex cream is so slippery, so thick," Amanda said, her voice smoky. She stirred her finger against my opening and worked another between my lips. Gently, she massaged the side of my clitoris.

Absorbed by overpowering sensations, I went crazy. I pulled my pussy lips apart, hoping Amanda would strum the engorged flesh.

"Amanda, don't stop. Please don't stop."

I ran my finger against my clit. The firm tissue felt like a tiny hard ball beneath the spongy folds.

Amanda pressed on. Her massaging fingers pinpointed the spot. Her fingers rubbed, then beat. She did not stop.

Amanda fell to her knees and wrapped my legs around her shoulders. Her lips found my clit — how could they not? I was so big, so hard. Her breath was hot on my pussy. Lightly first, her lips fluttered against my juice-soaked flesh. Then, with incredible precision, she pursed her lips around my clit-tip and blew so strongly that her lips vibrated remarkably fast. The sensation was violently arousing. Tremors of pleasure radiated from my central pleasure-point.

Amanda, her chin sugar-coated, looked at me with a self-satisfied smile. My sex-lips were stretched tightly between her fingers. My clit, tripled in size, jutted like a dark red mini-dome from the flushed, fleshy hood.

"Okay, sweet, fasten your seat belt," she said as she slipped an over-the-hand vibrator on.

Her entire hand immediately fired into a high-paced buzz. My cherry-colored pearl protruded desperately. She barely touched my clit yet currents shot through me.

I pulled her hair. I cried out. I ached from the unbearable teasing.

And she pressed her mouth on mine. She kissed me, hard — my cream all over her face, all over mine. She had me now.

Her expert fingers encircled my straining clit. They zoned in. They hummed in a thousand vibrations. Her fingers rippled, pulsating as they twisted and tapped my clitoris. I was sliding on heated velvet. I was diving in hot springs. A single bolt of lightning struck and I surrendered to her.

Floating in an intoxicating afterglow, I pulled Amanda closer to me. I wanted to kiss her, to touch her, to share the pleasure she had just given me.

"Amanda." I caressed her shoulders and back. "No one has ever taken the time to please me like you do."

"Is that so?" Amanda teased. She leaned to kiss me but was interrupted by the telephone's ringing. "Well?" She glanced toward the phone.

"Jason," I said with a sour expression.

"At some point you're going to have to deal with him."

I nodded reluctantly as Amanda answered the phone.

"Is she back?" I could hear Jason demand.

"Hello to you too, Jason," Amanda said sarcastically. Rolling her eyes, she passed me the phone.

"Yes, Jason," I said, dryly. "I'm back."

"Where the hell have you been? Do you have any idea how worried I've been? Running out like you did, not coming home, not calling."

"I was taking some time to think." I wanted to hang up. The push of one button and Jason would disappear.

"Come home now. We have to talk."

"I don't think I can do that right now," I said quietly. I braced myself for an avalanche of rage.

"What's that supposed to mean?" Jason snapped. "Is it her? You can't leave because of her?" His voice was uneven.

"No," I said decisively. "It's because of me. I need some time away."

"Just like before, is that it, Veronica?" Jason's voice grew louder and was beginning to cave into anger. "Found someone else and just like that, you're not interested in me anymore. Who's going to be there to pick up the pieces after you're through with your dyke girlfriend? Huh? Not me! Not this time!"

"Fine, Jason."

I hung up on him. The only emotion I felt was relief.

"Are you okay?" Amanda asked.

I nodded.

"Do you have to work tomorrow? Do you need to go back there tonight for clothes? We can go together," Amanda offered. "You're safe here. You can stay as long as you like. You know that, don't you?"

I took a moment to consider my options. I didn't want to go home to Jason. I could envision him as he paced the room, pressuring me for answers. *Why, Veronica? What next, Veronica?*

I had no answers for him. I had no answers for anyone. I didn't have to work tomorrow. I could stay with Amanda, give Jason a chance to cool down, give myself time to evaluate my next move.

"I don't want to go home tonight," I said emphatically. "Are you sure you don't mind?"

"My home is yours." Amanda hugged me. "What you need is to relax, dear lady. How about a nice hot bubble bath?"

"Yes, a bath," I said with a sigh.

Amanda headed for the bathroom. I heard the water as the tub filled.

"I'll get some Chinese food for us while you soak. How does that sound?" Amanda called.

"Why don't you take a bath with me?" I said, stretching.

"Barely enough room for one in here!" she laughed.

As I headed for the bath, I noticed the dream book open on the floor. The picture of the wolf beckoned to me. I knelt down, fascinated. Compelled to look directly into the wolf's insistent eyes, I felt immediately sucked into their bewitching shadows. Our eyes locked and a deep hunger passed through me.

I wait, impatient for you, Feronia. Climb in.

Had the wolf whispered?

Amanda returned to the living room. "Go ahead, climb in. The bath's ready."

I forced my eyes from the picture to Amanda. She was thumbing through the phone book.

"Sweet and sour sounds good or maybe spicy —"

"Anything," I said, distracted.

Again, I looked at the wolf. The eyes glared.

Yes, Feronia, climb in.

Something about those eyes — *her black eyes, shadowed in grays and lined with charcoals.* Something about those eyes — *reflecting the flames like burning embers.* I knew those eyes. Devana.

The wolf's eyes first glimmered, then burned. Now they seared. I had to go back.

"Be back in twenty," Amanda said with a smile. "Get in that bath and relax."

I closed the book and blew Amanda a goodbye kiss.

I knew my plan would upset Amanda, but I felt as if I had no choice. The wolf had beckoned me. Her eyes implored me to hurry back to the dream.

And really, what harm? What harm would there be in a light nap — perhaps twenty minutes — just to see, just to find out exactly what was so important about that wolf?

I looked at the picture. The eyes burrowed into me, stirred me, filled me with an unsettling longing. I had to go back. I had to go back now.

I skimmed the pages in search of the words Amanda had chanted to enter the dream world. A quiet desperation egged me on. There was nothing, no clue. I glanced at the clock. Amanda would be back soon. There wasn't enough time, not nearly enough time, to go through the book carefully, to siphon through all the information.

Perhaps if I waited for Amanda, explained how very much I wanted to go back, she would change her mind. It seemed hopeless. I went into the bedroom and fell across the bed with a disappointed sigh.

The room was dark, but gradually becoming more audible, I heard the gallop of the horse. I brought the book to my breast, as if to hang on — after all, the wind was so strong.

* * * * *

There is a rustling in the bushes. It is night and I am frightened.

"Who's there?" I call out into the darkness but there is no answer.

The moon is a pale crescent pinned to the black sky. A penetrating chill moves through me and I wonder where my fur cape is. I'm afraid that I won't be warm enough. I don't understand why I am alone.

Devana:
Sister To Wolves

Chapter 9

"She has come back to you. She waits in the woodland." Althea's words were low as she circled the fire. Her steel-bright eyes darted first to Devana and then to Lupina.

"Alone?" Devana watched Althea intently. Althea's straw-white hair, pulled back severely and knotted at the nape of her neck, reflected a golden glow. Wrapped in furs, she wore beaded leather straps on her slender wrist.

"Yes, alone. She is frightened," Althea said.

"And the other is not stumbling around,

searching for her?" Devana could feel Lupina's eyes beckon her, yet she kept her focus on Althea's beaded wrist.

"She has come in alone. I am certain." Althea hesitated, glancing at Lupina.

Devana's gaze drifted to Lupina. Firelight flickered in Lupina's auburn hair. Her eyes sparked with fury. Refusing to acknowledge Lupina's silent summons, Devana peered beyond her to the moon. "The moon is all but a splinter in the sky." Devana paused, contemplating its three-quarter shadow. "I must go to her." Considering how long Devana had waited for this moment, she felt surprisingly calm. "You are certain. The other has not come in with her," Devana said once more.

"She came in alone."

"Then I must hurry." Devana's voice was strong.

She gazed into the valley. The idea of movement coupled with the thrill of the run stirred the familiar push of energy inside of her. The power built quickly, surged through her, until it reached its sudden crescendo. Within seconds, Devana had transformed. Stretching her four legs, she howled to the carved moon.

Devana, sister to wolves, once again had married the darkness. Darting through the trees, she began her descent.

Lupina watched Devana slip into the night. She shot an angry glance to Althea who had been the bearer of this disturbing news.

"Well done, Althea," she growled sarcastically.

There was a distinct sharpness in her throat, and bitterness parched her mouth. She circled the campfire to Althea's side.

"You knew that this day would come to pass, Lupina." Althea's voice was guarded.

Lupina could sense Althea's wariness. Lupina, although one of the smaller in the tribe, possessed cunning ways and an unpredictable nature that made her one of the more dangerous.

"But who would have thought? Who could have imagined that after all this time she would return?" Lupina's voice trailed into silence. She stared out to the stars.

How difficult it was to see Devana so eager, Lupina thought, despondent. Not that she hadn't understood this was a possibility. Not that Devana hadn't made her longing for Feronia known. But to jump up, to hurry into the night — not even a glance, not so much as a word to Lupina?

Lupina had been cautioned that this day might eventually come. Devana herself had made that quite clear.

"You can run with me, comfort me, sleep at my side," Devana had said. "But someday, Feronia will return and reclaim her place at my side."

After countless moon phases had passed and Feronia's homecoming seemed less promising, Lupina's concerns had diminished. How foolish Feronia had been, Lupina had thought confidently. How frivolous Feronia's experiment with the herbs — jeopardizing her love, her status in the pack, to journey to an unknown world.

In Lupina's eyes, Feronia, with her implicit need for discovery, had abandoned Devana. Lupina was no

fool. After Feronia's disappearance, she had catered
to Devana's every need. A loyal and trustworthy
consort, Lupina had pampered Devana, had soothed
Devana, had excessively indulged and flattered
Devana. But for what? After all the love she had
lavished upon Devana, Devana had leapt from her
side and rushed into the night.

Lupina peered into the darkness and growled.
Devana had disappeared.

Devana raced through the night, bounding toward
Feronia. Approaching the woodland, she slowed her
pace, allowing the transformation to her woman-self
to begin. Once completed, Devana called, "Feronia?
Feronia?"

Devana came through the trees, into the small
clearing. Feronia sat on a tree stump, arms wrapped
around herself as if in a desperate attempt to keep
warm.

"Devana?"

"Yes, oh yes!" Devana shouted as she rushed to
Feronia. "My love, my precious, you have come back
to me!"

"I was so frightened. I was so alone, so cold."
She trembled in Devana's arms.

Devana removed her outer furs and wrapped
Feronia in them. The night was cold but it was
Feronia's comfort that concerned her now. The thick
vest and leggings she wore beneath the furs would
have to suffice. She briskly rubbed Feronia's arms to
warm her completely. "You came alone?" she asked.

Feronia nodded.

"I had hoped! I had willed that it be so!" Devana said quickly. She embraced her. "My Feronia, always the cunning one."

Feronia laid her head against Devana's shoulder and inhaled deeply.

"Come," Devana said. She lingered momentarily in Feronia's exotic midsummer fragrance. "I'll take you back to the shelter."

There was something about the ridge where Devana had found shelter — the vast sky embroidered with tiny stars; the small alcove where Veronica now sat wrapped in a blanket of furs that made her believe she'd been here before and stood at the edge of this cliff, had called out. Not once, but many times, hundreds of times she'd stood on the edge of the night and stared into the abyss, waiting for the precise moment.

Veronica tried to summon the memories that were teasing her. She was spellbound by the lone white moon-arc and had a sudden desire to stretch her legs and race through the trees.

"The stars have finally unmasked themselves." Laden with wood, Devana appeared from the trees.

Veronica shifted her eyes from the transfixing moon to watch Devana's swift, agile walk. The fur vest she wore revealed her muscular arms and the curve of her full breasts. Her legs were strong, her movements certain.

Silver beads and feathers, entwined on her leather necklace, jingled as Devana piled the wood inside a circle of stones. "You would always come to this cliff," she said. She glanced to Veronica then out to the sky. "From here you would start your descent."

Devana lit a twig and placed it under a branch. Blowing lightly on the small flame, she encouraged its power.

"My descent," Veronica said faintly. Watching the flames rise, the word *descent* tumbled lightly through her mind. In a fragmented vision, she was racing past trees. Her strong heartbeat, her rapid breath, matched the rhythm of her measured gait. "What is it about you?" Veronica turned to Devana. "When I'm awake, I feel things, sense things. Your eyes stare out at me from pictures. I hear you calling me."

"Don't you see?" Devana sat next to her. "You've felt me because I've been searching for you. I've called for you. You belong with me. *This* is your home. Out there, where you have been lost," Devana pointed to the star-studded sky, "is the dream, the fantasy world."

She pulled the fur high around Veronica's neck. "It's unfortunate that the passage has caused your memories to fade. When you first decided to journey, we knew this was a risk. But I vowed, by the blood of the first killed deer, if you were somehow immersed or lost, I would come after you and bring you back." Devana let out a long sigh. "Finding you has taken forever. You were swept way, inside the dream, out of my grasp. Thank the Goddess that the path presented itself."

"I don't understand," Veronica said, confused. "There are people who are waiting for me. I have a life and this is just a dream."

Veronica thought of Amanda. In the short time

they had known each other, they had become remarkably close. And Jason, her marriage, the life they had created together — she felt suddenly overwhelmed.

"I have faint recollections when I sit here with you," Veronica said, trying to find the logic in the situation. "But these are just dream memories, déjà vu, remnants from dreams long forgotten. Perhaps they resurface in a recent strong dream." Veronica shook her head and stood. The blanket of fur fell around her feet, leaving her chilled. "But a life here? With you? I don't remember a life."

"Then I will *make* you remember." Devana grabbed Veronica firmly. "I'll take you where the sights and scents will awaken you, once and for all. The heat of the run, the excitement of the chase, oh yes, you'll remember. *This* is your life, Feronia! *This* is your home!"

Dizzy, Veronica closed her eyes. She could barely hear the words yet the deep guttural tone of Devana's voice hypnotized her.

"Don't you worry, my uncertain companion," Devana uttered, her voice not unlike a growl. "You *will* remember."

Amanda:
The Nightmare

Chapter 10

"Veronica?" There was no answer. "Veronica?"

I set the Chinese food on the table and walked into the bedroom. No Veronica — not in the bathroom, not in the spare room, not in the kitchen. I hurried to the front door and stepped onto the porch. Yes, her car was there. I had thought it was there.

"Veronica!" I yelled into the night. Nothing.

Back into the bedroom, I clicked on the light. The book, opened and seemingly abandoned, was lying on the bed.

"Shit."

From the page, the wolf, whose expression was almost a gloat, stared back at me.

"Shit!" I tossed the book across the room. "Is this where you are? Goddamit, Veronica, is this where you are?"

I had no desire to go back into a dream. I had been out of control, out of my realm, during the last dream journey. Things had been more different than ever before, as though I had been demoted from director to a scant walk-on part.

Veronica should not have done this, I thought angrily. She had jeopardized herself, forcing us both into a precarious situation.

I went back to the porch.

"Veronica? Veronica!"

I had no alternative but to go after her. God only knew where she had ended up or what kind of danger she had exposed herself to. Damn her!

Returning to my bed, I sprinkled the contents of another dream bag onto the pillows. The bronze sculpture stared fixedly at me. *Not this time. Don't go. Don't go.*

I lay on my bed, closed my eyes, and began to chant.

I do not like this place. It is night and it is very cold. The bare moon gives a shallow light. There are two paths in front of me. I want to take the nearest path. It is wide and seems less treacherous than the other. But I know I have no choice.

The other path, my path, is covered with brush.

There is a machete on the ground. I need to cut through the overgrown path. I reach for the handle. A ferret leaps from the bush with a snarl and sinks its sharp fangs into my hand. I scream in horror. It has clamped onto my hand and won't let go. There is blood everywhere. I flail my hand attempting to knock loose the ferret but its teeth dig further. The pain is unbearable.

There is foam around the ferret's mouth. His eyes are glazed. I am certain he is diseased. I know the disease will enter my body and will make me crazy. I grab the machete and slash the ferret to no avail. The disease burns through my hand then my wrist as it travels up my body. Screaming in agony, I hack at my arm.

"No! No!"

I woke up screaming in panic. Alone in the bed, the room pitch-black, I lunged forward, wildly feeling for my arm.

A dream. A dream. A dream. A dream, the darkness seemed to whisper.

I clicked on the light. Only a nightmare, I told myself. The light made things safe. Only a nightmare, the dark remnants from the dream dissolved.

With a relieved sigh, I closed my eyes only to be confronted by a haunting vision of Veronica, on the edge of a cliff, calling to me. I bolted forward, my heart slamming in my chest.

"Veronica!" I leaped out of bed and searched the house again. "Veronica!"

She hadn't returned. There was no doubt in my mind where she was. My life, out of the dream, was fast becoming a nightmare in itself.

Where was Veronica and why couldn't I get to her?

I made several attempts to go back to the dream world. I tried to relax, tried to fall into a dream, but every time I closed my eyes, I'd get the troubling vision, fleeting and transitory, of Veronica and nothing more. I could see her in the dark and then she'd be gone.

Suddenly denied access to the dream world, I searched the book, hoping to find information that would guide me. I found nothing.

I flipped to the picture of the wolf. My words, *always the wolves,* were scribbled below. The wolf peered back at me with a savage glare that seemed eerily protective.

"You," I said accusingly. "It's you, isn't it? You have her trapped somewhere."

I read the caption beneath the picture. *The wolf may be a symbol of the dream traveler herself. Like the wolf, the traveler may be entranced by the Goddess of the Night.*

Goddess of the Night . . . Goddess of the Night . . . I thumbed to the index in hopes of finding something more.

There was nothing. What else? What else? I scanned the index for a suggestion. Perhaps if I let go, a word, a clue of some sort would jump out at me. I slid my finger down the columns of words. Nothing until, as I passed over one, a small chill passed through me. *Devana: page 62.*

Devana. Devana. Hadn't Veronica said that name? I turned to the page.

Devana, Woodland Moongoddess, whose priestesses wore the masks of hunting dogs; whose mad Votaries donned the fur of wolves and raced beside her in the night. Mother of Creatures, Devana gave birth to all animals. Yet paradoxically, as huntress, she is killer of those she brought forth.

Killer of those she brought forth.

I grabbed three dream bags and fell onto the bed.

"Please, please, I must find her. Take me to Devana. Take me to Devana."

The room was quiet. Taking in the scent of the herbs, I thought of the cliff where I had envisioned Veronica. I imagined climbing the long, steep path to get to her.

Devana. Devana. Devana. I began the chant.

"She has a way about her, you know."

"Like hypnotism?" I watch the owl carefully.

"If you are implying a loss of one's personal power, I'd have to disagree with that particular word. It's all in her presentation," the owl replies.

Lifting a wing over his head, the owl bursts into a ball of flames. Using the light from the fire, I open the book of symbols. The owl symbolizes the dead sun.

I do not care that the owl has gone. I know not to trust anyone. I reach to my belt and touch the sharp dagger I have brought with me. I feel safe.

"And if you think a dagger will take her down, will overpower her . . ."

I turn quickly. The owl is now sitting on the branch of a different tree. It stares down with mock concern.

". . . then you might as well have a seat and wait, for her consorts will surely tear you to shreds."

"Is that so! Do you think I'm frightened? Is that what you think?" I yell at the owl.

"I certainly hope so," the owl says with a self-satisfied smirk. He nonchalantly spreads his wings, lifts into the air and, without another word, vaporizes.

I walk down the path. It is sunrise. The woods are quiet. The sun breaks forth with life. The sun is my companion. I see a lake. A lone white horse wades in the water. A bell is tied around its neck.

The horse sees me approaching and hurries out of the lake. Water splashes everywhere. The bell begins to ring loudly.

The telephone's demanding ring woke me from the dream.

"I need to speak with Veronica." It was Jason. His gruff voice was intrusive and I pulled the phone slightly back from my ear.

"Veronica is busy," I said, aggravated that his call had severed me from my dream.

"Don't start that with me, Amanda," he said angrily. "Tell her to get on the phone now."

"That's really impossible, Jason." I tried to sound calm. The last thing I wanted was Jason's involvement. I had made progress in the dream. With a little more time, a few more journeys . . .

"I don't think you get it, Amanda. Veronica is my wife. We have a history, a life together. Far beyond that, we're friends, companions. I can't imagine her cutting me off in this way, not speaking to me. This is because of you, your influence."

"Jason, please," I said, my voice fading. How long would he accept that Veronica was simply unwilling to come to the phone? "It's not as though she's been hypnotized."

"Put her on the phone, goddamit, or I'm coming after her!"

"Maybe later," I muttered. "She'll call you later."

"This is a fucking nightmare!" Jason slammed down the phone.

And in that moment, Jason and I were in unhappy agreement.

As I unsuccessfully attempted to return to the dream, urgent banging on the front door startled me. Placing the dream book on the nightstand, I hurried to the living room. Praying it was Veronica, hoping she had returned, I opened the front door.

"Veronica?"

"Where is she, Amanda?" Jason pushed into my house.

"Jason?"

I was trembling. I regretted that I hadn't looked out the window to confirm who was at my door.

"If she's not here, then where the hell is she?" Jason swung around. He was taller than I had imagined, with a strong build. His disheveled hair looked as though he had been running his fingers through the thick black curls.

"Like I tried to explain to you on the phone . . ." I hoped that by speaking slowly I'd quiet my pounding heart and create some semblance of tranquility. "She'll call you later. When she gets in."

"And where is she?" He sneered. "Her car is here, but she's not?"

And what could I say — that I had lost her? That she had fallen asleep and was stolen from me, stolen from him, in a dream?

"The dream," I barely whispered. "I lost her in a dream."

Jason just stood there. The anger on his face faded to perplexity. "Lost in a dream, huh?" He spoke in a patronizing tone as if he were trying to find the child who had broken the picture window and I had referred him to an imaginary friend.

"A dream," I replied carefully.

There was nothing else to do but to tell him, I conceded. Otherwise he would wait for her to come back. Valuable time would be wasted. There was no time to spare. Veronica was trapped in the dream world, perhaps a prisoner of the Huntress of the Night.

I decided to tell Jason the truth. He could draw his own conclusions. As far as I was concerned, Veronica needed me, needed me now. And if he so chose, Jason — admittedly not the most likely of dream companions — was welcome to help bring her home.

Feronia:
The Homecoming

Chapter 11

My hand in hers, Devana led me down a path. As we moved away from the fire, I was surprised by how well my eyes adjusted to the dark. We descended the side of the mountain and I watched Devana as she moved ahead. She had a confidence, a oneness with the night, that mesmerized me.

The grove we entered, surrounded by a fortress of trees, was impenetrably dark. Even so, my sight had become keen. The field spread before us like a blanket of tall grass. Although the colors eluded me, a collage of scents burst into a mirage of greens, yellows and purples. Filled with the subtle sound of movement, the pitch-black meadow seemed alive.

Devana turned toward me. Without the fire's reflection, her eyes still appeared burnt-orange, as though radiating an internal flame.

With a sweep of her hand, Devana motioned to the entire clearing. "It is here where we last bonded. On that night, the moon was bursting from the charcoal sky. Do you not remember?"

Captivated by the glow of Devana's red-yellow eyes, I stood motionless. The wind swept through the trees with a lonely whistling sound.

"Uncertain of the journey that lay ahead, you held onto me so tightly," Devana murmured. "I didn't want you to go. I told you this countless times. But my Feronia, my dream traveler, my explorer of mystical labyrinths, had her destiny to pursue."

Devana's breath was hot against my cheek. "Our love has been tested by your journey. The time has passed too slowly. How many fortnights I have watched the pregnant moon give birth to empty darkness!"

Devana pushed her fingers through my hair. A primitive heat escaped from her hands and passed into me. A vague recollection teased me. Pouring from the full moon, silver light had cascaded across this very clearing. I had lain naked on the soft grass with Devana and kissed her drawn-tight, ebony nipples.

I swirled in reeling memories, staggering visions of Devana and me in this grove. Barely covered in scraps of fur, we had danced wildly. Black shadows surrounded us in a frenzied circle. The quiet night was severed only by our serenade to the moon. The forest had echoed with wild, hollow baying.

"I'm frightened," I whispered to Devana. The wind's mournful song had temporarily subsided. In the stillness, each sound seemed extraordinarily magnified. There was a subtle rustling in the forest. Slight footsteps stole through the dark. We were not alone. I could feel their eyes, between the trees, watching us. The wind let out another lonely howl.

My pulse quickened. "I should go home now. After I wake up, I'll take some time to —"

Devana began to lick my neck. Her heart beat furiously as she pushed her breasts against mine.

"You *are* home. You *are* awake," Devana said, her voice strong.

Her mouth became more insistent. Kissing my neck, she pulled the fur cape from my shoulders. Her tongue lashed repeatedly. A wet trail of saliva cooled against my skin.

Her fragrance was sultry — the cape slipped from my shoulders. Her wildness tantalized me — the cape fell. Her kisses were fire-tainted — my knees sank to the soft fur as we plummeted to the ground.

A small, indistinct voice called from the trees. *Come home, Veronica. Come home.* But my body rebelled with an instinctive urge to stay. The voice didn't matter. Nothing mattered except Devana's spark-showering kisses.

There were others dancing behind us, or was it a vision? Silhouettes blended with trees. Trees danced with shadows. Opened, my eyes saw only darkness. Closed, they saw flames.

Devana's mouth darted heat across my shoulder

to my armpit. Her teeth clasped the sensitive skin and pinched it sharply. I moaned involuntarily. Those bites — I had sudden flashes of having had this very sensation on my breasts, on my belly, between my legs.

"You remember now, don't you?" Devana panted. "You and I, in this very grove — oh how the moon bathed us in a veil of silver light!"

Devana bit the curve of my breast. Her sharp nails scraped jagged strokes the full length of my back.

I did not resist, had no desire to resist. The small voice from moments before was lost beneath the intent sound of Devana's passion-filled growls. I cared to go nowhere except where Devana wanted to lead me. It was Devana I wanted, Devana I craved. Untamed Devana — her coarse scent, her sharp bite, her cutting nails — unleashed a wild-animal hunger within me.

"Oh, Devana, yes, Devana." I was flooded with memories of her mouth sucking my breasts.

Tempting her to latch onto my thickened nipple, I arched my back. My eyes opened and shadows danced in a black-spinning circle. My eyes closed and the dancers' feet beat the ground in feverish rhythm. Devana and I were prisoners in a dark-spinning vortex, and the air trembled with a frenetic buzz.

Devana's lips found my throbbing nipple. Pressing tightly, she slowly sucked.

"Not enough." I twisted beneath her.

Devana's sucking intensified and my nipple stretched tight in her mouth. Pleasure-heat bolted to my clitoris. I reached between my legs. Moisture had seeped from my fur-lined lips and my upper thighs were slippery. Dipping my finger between the flaccid, cleaved folds, I nudged my slick clit. Devana alternately bit and sucked my burning nipple. Delirious, I pleaded for more.

The dancers whirled and a hot current of air heightened the fervor of the spinning circle. Wild growling crescendoed and I smelled untamed scents as they reeled around us in a black, churning, passion-charged wheel.

Devana burrowed between my legs. She nipped my thighs, covering me with sharp, delicious bites. Hungry with anticipation, I stroked my sex until it gaped.

"Open to me. Let me all the way into you, Feronia," Devana coaxed. It was as if the shadows were pleading.

I separated my thick lips for her. I wanted her between them. I wanted to smother her in my pussy. The air she sucked would come from my cunt. She would breathe me. I would be her.

"That's it, my sister, my shadow, my mate. Let me in, let me in," Devana hissed. Her words slipped against my soaked flesh.

"Devana! Yes. Take me."

The night was abruptly thrust into motionless silence. The dancers were trees. The trees were shadows. The only sound was the slight click the satin-pearl wetness on my vagina made as Devana shoved her tongue into me.

Her rigid tongue sank in. Past the protective slit-muscles that attempted to resist her, past the roughened tissue that hung across the opening like a pink guard, her tongue pierced the space between my tight vaginal walls. She forced them to yield with her insistent tongue-thrusts.

Once in, once she opened me, she wiggled her tongue teasingly and then pulled out slowly. I tried to clamp her thick tongue between the partitions of flesh, to hold her in longer, but she withdrew. I whimpered. More, I wanted more.

She gradually pried her tongue back in, then dragged it out. Over and over, she pushed then pulled. I was rising. My entire body pounded with tension. I grabbed her hair. I wanted it faster, harder.

Devana stopped. She looked at me. Her eyes were aflame and her lips were coated with white honey.

"No, please," I begged. I wanted her tongue back in me.

"Say it," Devana said, her voice low, intent. "Say your name."

Come back into me, my hips demanded. I craved her touch. What had she said to me? Why had she stopped?

"Your name, Feronia, let me hear you say your name."

My name, my name, my name. Fragments, like clips from a movie, flashed in my mind — *Come home, Veronica. Where are you, Veronica?* My body was burning with desire.

"Your name. Say your name."

"Feronia," I whispered. The word swirled in my ears.

"Shout it! Into the night!" Devana cried. With a

surge of power, she turned me onto my hands and knees.

"Oh yes, oh yes," I screamed. "Feronia."

She tapped her fingers against my thick-ribbed slit. "And your home is . . . ?"

I moaned as I thrust my ass in the air. Push them in. Push them in, Devana.

"And your home is . . . ?" Devana repeated. She barely inserted the tips of her fingers.

"With you," I cried. "My home is here, with you."

A hard push and she was in. My body jerked, overwhelmed by her. I had forgotten how thick and large her fingers were. She penetrated me with an exactness that was certain. Motionless, she did not move. Instead, she held her fingers completely still. How perfectly her fingers filled me!

Devana. My love, my lover, Devana. Take me. Darkness burst into the red fire of desire. I opened my eyes to plead for more but stealthy movements in the distance alerted me.

The trees now stood regal and shadows loomed in slow approach. Devana fluttered her fingertips as if to call me back. But in the dark, the sound of cautious footsteps, unmistakably distinct, held my attention.

Devana pushed her hand in front of my eyes and plunged deeper into me. In the sudden darkness, blinded by the pleasure of her continued thrusting, I dismissed the shadows. As I lunged toward her prying fingers, she sank into me, burrowed into me, into my deep-seated pleasure-points.

And then there were hands, hot hands, on my

breasts, against my back, in my hair. Brazen mouths were kissing me. Quivering tongues were licking me. Sharp nails scraped me as Devana continued on with her delicious thrusting. Jabbing into me, she infiltrated all my secret places.

She was behind me, then she wasn't. She was next to me, in front of me, beneath me. But the fingers kept pushing in. More and more fingers drove into my throbbing crevice. I pressed my face into the grass and attempted to raise my ass even higher. Hands held my hips up. Hands separated my ass.

"You are home. You are home," Devana, at my side, whispered over and over.

Slow penetrations, fast penetrations. It was one, then another. My eyes opened and flames surrounded me. My eyes closed and shadows stalked me.

Shadows with eyes that glimmered like orange embers were taking me. Their hands pawed me, covered me, grabbed me. Nails cut into my flesh. I was wet with blood, wet with sweat, wet with sex. I arched for more but instead they turned me onto my back.

One held each leg and they stretched me apart. A shadow straddled my face and I was submerged in her sopping fur. Her scent was intoxicating. I was drunk. I was euphoric.

"Welcome home, mistress." Devana's words penetrated the musky darkness.

The nails cut deep. Fingers, tongues, hands pushed up and down my breasts, my belly, my aching cunt.

I was blinded by the shadow's sex. I was lost in her fleshy folds. She slid back and forth across my face until I was swathed in a sticky milk-glaze.

They were chanting words I couldn't understand. The shadow blended into the whirling black circle. Above me, Devana held a steaming wooden bowl.

Shadows pinned my arms and legs against the ground while Devana spilled the aromatic elixir first into my mouth and then onto my spread-wide vulva. Almost too warm, the liquid sloshed onto me. The sharp taste of mint was strong. My head began to spin. My clitoris tingled as though tiny heated beads were rapidly increasing in speed on the swollen, meaty flesh. Thousands of vibrations shot from my clit into my vagina. Unlike anything, fire raged through my womb and I exploded into thunderous release.

The thunder shattered into silence. The shadows stood above and Devana was at my side.

"Welcome home, Feronia," she growled.

And the shadows began to howl.

Paws scraped the dirt. Figures moved in the distance. From woman to wolf, Devana had shifted. Watching me closely, her flame-orange eyes peered from the darkness. Although her dark coat was sprinkled with shades of gray, her muscular legs were ebony. Imposing yet graceful, she circled me. Her body was sleek. Her movements were strong. Strangely beautiful — my Devana, wolf-woman, lover for all times.

"Let go, Feronia. Fall into the spell." She had not spoken yet I could hear her thoughts. The sweet scent of anticipation filled the air.

The other wolves encircled us. With their long snouts raised in the air, they paced impatiently. Howling, almost moaning, their haunting cries cut the night.

"You will run with us as we honor your return."

Turning away, Devana began a slow trot. The others hurried to her side.

"Come, Feronia."

A strange dizziness consumed me. My vision blurred. Devana, surrounded by wolves, moved up and down in undulating waves.

"Don't leave me, Devana. Take me with you, Devana!" I pleaded.

The waves were plunging. Devana was far ahead. The wolves disappeared into the trees.

"Devana!"

Fighting the waves, hungry to catch up with her, I climbed to my feet. The trees flowed to the sky. The stars descended to the ground. I struggled to reorient myself.

You are home — voices whispered and I stood firm. *You are ready* — I held my ground against the waves. *Come with us* — the power of the waves, surging through me, became mine.

The trees and stars had settled and the night was suddenly quiet. Calling to the dark sky, I was exhilarated when singing howls echoed back.

On all fours, I broke into a long-legged gait to join the pack. I was home.

Amanda: The Swiftness Of The Deer

Chapter 12

"I don't like this either," I said, my voice cold. "Believe me, the last person I want in my bed is you!"

"Don't start getting smart-ass with me, Amanda." Jason sat next to me on the bed. "This cock and bull story —"

"Look, Jason," I cut in. "Like I told you before, you have a choice. Whether you believe me or not is not my problem. I don't have time to sit here bullshitting with you. I've got to get to Veronica."

I grabbed several dream bags and lay back. "You

said you were in. Fine, Jason, you're in. Just don't start up with me."

Jason gave me a sarcastic look and then lay next to me. "So how does this voodoo crap work?"

Shooting Jason a nasty look, I sat up. "One more asshole comment and I swear, you're fucking out of here."

"Okay, okay, I'm sorry," Jason said apologetically. He pulled me back down. "So what's next?"

"We have to hold each other. I chant certain words. We have to fall asleep in each others arms."

"Okay, that's enough!" Jason sprang to a sitting position. "Where the hell is she? Is this some sort of a kinky scene you've convinced her to participate in?"

"Out!" I leapt off the bed. "Get out right now!" I flung open the bedroom door. "I don't need this shit! Do you hear me? I don't need this shit!"

Furious, I motioned for him to leave. Jason swung his legs over the side of the bed.

It was then, in that moment, that I heard the whispering. I looked directly at Jason's mouth and tried to decipher what he was saying, yet his lips weren't moving. He was staring at me, a blank expression on his face. I could hear the voice distinctly yet Jason seemed oblivious.

Yes, come in. Come in alone and her consorts will lift you in the darkness, will carry you off into the night. She will cut into you, pull you to shreds, devour you like the fresh-killed deer.

A dark fear pulsed through me. Was a grave danger awaiting me, perhaps even hungering for me, in the dream world? Suddenly, I didn't want to go in alone.

"We have to sleep with each other?" Jason said quietly. A solemn tone shadowed his voice as if my fear had somehow entered him and broken his skepticism.

I nodded.

"This is dangerous?" he asked.

We lay next to each other without a word.

We are in a valley. It is sunny yet the air is brisk. Jason is wearing a bandanna around his neck and a confident look on his face.

He walks toward me. I notice the deep purple berries he is carrying. They appear ready to burst, as though the juice can barely be contained in their thin skins.

"There are berries by the lake," he says. His lips are stained violet.

I am not hungry but I crave the coolness of the berries against my tongue. I take a handful and drop three berries in my mouth.

"Intoxicating," Jason says.

Laughing, I sit down. Yes. They are intoxicating.

A butterfly drifts to my shoulder. It flutters near my ear.

"They trick you with the berries," the butterfly whispers. She flits to my other ear. "They trick you with the berries."

I look at Jason. He is whirling in circles. His fingers and lips appear bruised from the stains.

"And indeed, they are bruises," says the butterfly. Caught by a breeze, she leaves a flurry of colored dust as she floats toward the sun.

Jason still spins in circles. I cannot tell if the blue-red marks on his arms are bruises or berry stains. He is whirling too fast. I need to stop him and examine the marks.

"Jason?" I try to stand but I am drunk.

I crawl to him. He stumbles onto me and falls to the ground. His arms are covered with leeches.

"They will suck you dry!" I shout, shaking him.

"What? Berry stains?" he says, laughing. His teeth are stained blue.

I do not understand. I reach for another berry but they are gone.

I look beyond him, to the sun, then glance to the mountain that looms in the near distance. On a steep ledge, staring down at us, stands a dark wolf.

"What?" I pushed Jason away. He was shaking me, forcing me out of a delicious dream.

"You left me behind! You left me behind!" Jason shouted.

I opened my eyes to find Jason above me, out of control, his eyes focused on mine. I tried to pull myself out of the haze.

"We were together." Jason stumbled over the words. "We were in this field eating berries and then I woke up. I couldn't get back. You were moaning and tossing in your sleep. I was afraid to leave you in there alone."

I sat up, now more awake. It was then that I saw them. I screamed. Jason's arms were covered with deep purple bruises.

* * * * *

"I just don't know," I said, frustrated.

Tossing the dream book on the couch, I watched Jason pace the living room. Haphazardly, he ran his fingers through his thick hair.

"Tell me you're giving up. Say those words and I swear —" Jason glared at me.

"I'm not giving up," I said vehemently. "But I'm worried. This is different than it's ever been." I covered my face with my hands. Things had gone wrong, very wrong. "I can't get back in. I'm blocked at the entrance." I shook my head. "And the bruises . . . Things are out of control."

"What the hell have you done," Jason said desperately, as though he had read my thoughts. He picked up the dream book and began thumbing through it. "Involving Veronica in dangerous games that you don't have any idea how to control." He slammed the book shut. "And you! You've wreaked havoc on everyone's life. For what? A weekend fling? A selfish experiment? And *suddenly* Amanda's blocked! *Suddenly* Amanda can't get back in," Jason sputtered in a mocking voice. "Veronica's my wife. Do you understand that concept? Mine. So don't give me shit about how you can't find her. If you don't, I will." Jason tossed the book at me and headed for the bedroom.

"She's *yours*?" I screamed. "Yours? Have you ever taken the time to really see who the hell she is? Why do you think she was so willing to be with me? Oh, she's fucking yours, all right." I grabbed his shoulder and looked him in the eye. "Understand

121

this, Jason. *I* will get Veronica back, if it's the last thing I do."

"Okay," I looked up from the dream book. "I think I've got something here. Butterfly —"

"Butterfly? We're back to the butterfly?" Jason said wearily. He leaned against the couch and rubbed his forehead.

"— is a symbol of the soul." I continued reading.

"Yeah," he said, obviously frustrated. "We already established that."

"It also symbolizes an unconscious attraction to the light." I took a moment to reconsider this information.

"So?" He seemed uncertain of my point.

After Jason's earlier outburst of anger, we had declared a truce for Veronica's sake. Analyzing the dream's images, we had spent the last hour searching for answers. "Perhaps the bruises were a map," Jason had said. "Or maybe the leeches meant sucking, that we should suck the berries, not eat them." His suggestions had become more farfetched with each passing minute and I had begun to wonder if dialogue with him was a help or a hindrance.

"Remember what we read about the wolf?" I said, as if speaking to a child. I was exemplifying incredible tolerance. "The Goddess of the Night?"

"The point, Amanda. Get to the damn point."

God, he was on my nerves.

"We need to dream about the butterfly. The butterfly can lead us —"

"Where in the hell did you come up with that?" Jason interjected angrily, on the verge of losing his temper again.

I wondered how Veronica could stand him.

"Is that what the book says, Amanda?" He grabbed the book. "I don't see anything about that in here. Why not berries, Amanda? Or leeches? Or the fucking bruises?" he said sarcastically. "Only expert Amanda's idea are worth anything, right?" He tossed the book back on the table.

Why yes, I thought cynically. The jerk and I were finally in agreement.

"The wolf is darkness." Ignoring his tantrum, I tried to keep my voice calm. "The butterfly attracts light. Maybe it's a metaphor. We fight the wolf with the butterfly. It represents hope, our only hope. Can't you see what I'm saying?"

"And what, sweetheart, are you saying? That we go in armed with a butterfly, for God's sake?"

I shot him a don't-fuck-with-me icy glare. "I'm not your fucking sweetheart. You want to start shit with me again, Jason? Huh?"

"Okay, okay," he mumbled.

"We've gone over and over this." I sighed. "There's nothing else left."

"Okay," Jason agreed reluctantly.

"Then it's settled. We go for the butterfly."

After all, there was no other alternative but to arm ourselves with hope.

I cannot believe how hot it is. It is midday and I am in a meadow. Birds sing and the sky is as silver as a sun-soaked lake. I have a butterfly net and a large beaded bag.

There is a splashing sound behind me. Jason dives into a crystal pond. The water rises above him and he disappears. The splash turns into a swarm of bees that quickly form the letter D in the air. The sound of the buzzing is incredibly loud. The sky has darkened.

I remember something about the butterfly and bring the net close to my breast. I cannot see Jason and wonder where he has gone. The bees are circling in the sky.

Jason climbs out of the water and is covered with honey. I want to take a finger-full into my mouth. I think that it will make me drunk so I say to Jason, "No way we eat the honey."

A butterfly appears from the center of the bees and soars down to my ear.

"Yes, eat the honey," the butterfly says. "The honey is okay."

Jason is smiling. I dip my finger in the honey and swirl the thick warmth into my mouth. I feel suddenly lightheaded.

"It will soon be very dark," says the butterfly. "The bees have a way of covering the whole sky. When the dark comes, watch for the wolves. That is when their hunt begins."

I turn to Jason. He has no teeth and his lips are very yellow.

There is a deep humming sound as the bees weave darkness into the light. The sky is almost completely blackened and the air is chilly. Jason is damp and shivering cold. I must search for shelter.

I enter the forest. There is barely any light and I

wonder how I will see. I no longer hear the bees and think that I am lost. I want to scream for help but am immobilized. I remember this feeling. I want to force my legs to walk. I have work to do and Jason is freezing.

Like an irradiated cloud, a life-sized glistening of yellow, blue and green fluorescence glistens in the trees ahead. I hurry toward the radiance but it eludes me by slipping through the trees.

"Please," I call. It teases me with the promises of light and heat.

Following the luminescence deeper into the forest, between tall redwood trees, up narrow paths, I stumble over rocks and bushes.

"Please," I cry, panting.

Abruptly, the silhouette stops and waits in a glimmer of powdered rhinestone light. I race, out of breath, to the place where the glowing has finally come to rest. It is here that she turns to me and spreads her glittering wings like a kimono as she whispers my name.

Beautiful, shimmering, she stands as tall as I. Her sapphire eyes twinkle. Carbon-black hair falls loosely to her shoulders. Her face and body are human yet large incandescent butterfly wings rise from behind her. Slowly, she opens her wings and showers me in a brilliant haze of rainbow dust. I sense she will take me into her and shelter me from the menacing cloak of darkness.

"Amanda." Almost singing, her voice is like silken flower petals misted with pastels.

I watch her mouth as she says my name. Preoccupied with her cherry-silver lips, her deep pink tongue, I wonder how many flowers she has sipped sweet nectar from. Her perfect mouth appears sticky as though thinly coated with honey-sap from the fields.

She steps closer and her fragrance sweeps me into a vision of lilacs, bluebells and lilies. She lightly kisses me and her lips are satin rose petals. Tasting the floral sugar of her mouth, I fall into sweet ambrosia.

She wraps her wings around me and I am blanketed in colors. We are spinning, or so it seems. Wanting to soar across the fields of flowers, to lie on glossy petals, to bathe in the heat of the sun, I am spellbound.

But there is no sun and Jason is cold. The butterfly encases me as she swirls in circles.

"Oh no," I mutter. "I must go to Jason. We have work."

The spinning suddenly stops. The butterfly steps back and stares at me intently. "Don't you see, Amanda?" she says seductively, her eyes hooded with flower dust. "This is the work. I will take you where you need to go. Your companion, a most unlikely choice, is sleeping under a blanket of furs. He cannot help you on your journey. Tell me you didn't foresee that in the beginning?"

And was she not right? I had a fragmented picture of Jason— had he eaten the berries? — sleeping near a rock, covered in furs.

"He will sleep safely until you have met your fate."

"My fate?" I ask, dizzy. More fragments swirl in my mind. I wonder if the dew that has passed from her lips to mine is a potion.

Her wings, like sparkling thin veils, close around

me. She draws me to her. Softness and exotic perfumes, she is a golden field-mermaid. I have lost my ability to reason. She has me in her powdered lightness and I do not care. The darkness of the night has dissolved.

Naked, wrapped in her fluorescent cape, I am soaring with her in a radiant heat. We reach a thick cloud and she lays me down. I am suspended in the billowy sky-pillow. She floats above me. Her wings rise and fall in a starburst of iridescence. A sprinkling of glitter drifts around me. Each crystal sends a rush of pleasure through me as it melts into a gem of color against my skin.

"Amanda, Amanda," she says alluringly. Her lips open to reveal her pink tongue.

Hovering above me, she flirts and flaunts her dazzling beauty. The colored flakes fall against my skin and their heat intensifies to a slight stinging. I am electric. I want her against me. I crave the radiance of her embrace and hunger for her charged power to enter my soul.

"You must become one with the night. Blend into the forest," she says. Her voice is deep blue velvet.

Staring into her indigo eyes, I see the reflection of the glimmering oasis of amber-blue that surrounds us.

"Who you seek has married the darkness and roams the wind-swept ridges." The butterfly still flutters above me. A sharp edge has invaded her words. "The sagacious owl journeys through the night unnoticed; the confident ferret steals through the underbrush unheard; but it is the deer who will take you to her."

The beat of her wings is steady, rhythmic. A

snowfall of rhinestone confetti swirls around me. I am clouded in a storm of glitter. I open my mouth to call to her but the rainbow crystals fall into my mouth and I cannot speak.

"She will come to you." I hear the butterfly, her voice distant, lost somewhere in the shimmering haze. "But you must first enter the night, swift and agile as the deer."

I taste the confection of the sparkling dust as it fills my mouth. I float, then tumble, spinning wildly, down, down, down into the heart of the dream. Crashing through barriers, hurling through colors that whirl about me, shadows call my name.

"Enter the night. She waits for you. Go to her, hurry to her! You must eat the glitter dust. Swallow it. Take it into you. The only way to bring her to you is with the surefootedness of the deer, the elusiveness of the deer, the swiftness of the deer. Swallow the dust, Amanda."

My mouth is full of the sparkling flakes and I have no choice. I swallow the colored power and my body begins to tremble.

Slamming against the ground, I am momentarily stunned. I have fallen into a clearing. Stark, foreboding mountains stare down at me. I force myself to stand then realize I am on four legs.

I sense shadows high on the mountain ridges, stealing between the trees. I feel a sudden vulnerability. Peering up at the jagged ridges, perking my ears, I listen to the night which is alive with the sound of small animals rustling about in the fields.

She is up there, somewhere, roaming the ridges. She is a prisoner of the darkness and I must bring her back.

Wobbling at first, I take a few small steps, until, finally sure of myself, I quicken to a graceful gait. In the guise of the deer, I head to the base of the dark mountains and become one with the night.

The Wolves

Chapter 13

She has come. She has come. She has come.

The words are whispered through the darkness.
From the lake, across the clearings, into the valleys,
up steep paths, behind large rocks, to the edge of
the precipitous ridges themselves — the whole forest
is murmuring in the night.

She has come. She has come. She has come.

Tonight the rabbits and squirrels, usually close to
the brush and safely camouflaged, are taking risks.
Tonight they wander in full view.

She has come. She has come. She has come.

And tonight, the hunt will be a ceremony, a sacrificial rite, that honors Feronia's return. How long since there has been a celebration! How long has it been since the wolves have turned their blood-red eyes from the smaller creatures to the highly prized deer?

She has come.

Chapter 14

The wolves raced through the hills, running up overgrown paths, crisscrossing through the night. Feronia was filled with incredible exhilaration. The wind, whipping against her face, parched her eyes with its coldness.

Not a noise was unheard, not a scent went unnoticed. Attuned with each step, each movement, her senses were alive, alerting her. A jackrabbit had passed here, a woodthrush had nested there. She could smell sweet water from the streams. She could hear the snowy owl flit across the sky.

There was nothing that compared to the sensations. Cutting through the night, slowing to a trot, nose to the ground, Feronia would then break into a swift run.

Surrounded by companions, they briefly separated, climbed different paths, then called out to each other. Their lone songs stirred the darkness. The smaller creatures scurried for cover as the continual howls reverberated in the night.

They entered a valley and the pack split apart once again. Devana sat off to one side while the other wolves circled Feronia. A large black wolf entered the circle, challenging Feronia with a growl. Although her status was widely recognized, Feronia had to engage in a symbolic confrontation to reestablish her seniority.

Baring her teeth, the large wolf lunged toward Feronia. Feronia leapt forward and clawed the wolf. They tumbled to the ground. Each took the other's skin between her teeth as though to pierce the flesh, yet they brought forth no blood. Growling and wrestling in the grass, they sparred in ritual challenge.

The dark wolf tried to overpower Feronia. Her teeth, dagger-like, were precariously close to tearing into Feronia's neck.

Had she forgotten? Feronia thought, caught off guard. Does she not realize that this is a symbolic display honoring my return and nothing more?

In her scent, in her breath, there was a wild desperation about the wolf. As though she wanted more than mere participation in the rite, the wolf seemed seriously intent to claim Feronia's place in the pack.

With razor-edged teeth against her neck, Feronia wondered if blood had indeed been drawn. Did the others not see this? Did they not care?

Feronia fought to straddle the wolf and lock her firmly against the ground. The wolf's struggle was violent, as if she had no intention of being defeated. Rage filled Feronia. Who was this? Had she no idea who Feronia was? In a final show of strength, Feronia pinned her down and howled with masterful certainty, "I am Feronia. Goddess of the Night. Consort to Devana!"

The circle broke, joyous with evident relief. Feronia, swept in triumphant glory, no longer cared why the challenge had been so decidedly realistic.

Chapter 15

Tonight it is the deer — the blood of the fresh-killed deer: a hunt rare, honored, a ritual of the highest order. The wolves respect the deer — her beauty, her uncompromising docility — and most often restrict their nightly rounds to the smaller, more bothersome of the night creatures. The quivering field mouse, with its predictable ways and loathsome habits, offers a meager and flavorless meal. The rabbit, after a tiresome chase, is ordinary fare. But on this occasion, the deer becomes the trophy.

The wolves remember another ceremony, long ago, when the scent of the deer was tracked in the night air. They had prowled through the trees, to the base of the mountains, into the clearings. Mouths damp with anticipation, they had thirsted for the sweet kill.

It was the night when Feronia had chosen to leave the others behind. On a journey to the land of visions, she had taken the mixture of leaves and berries and vanished into the night.

She had vowed to return but time moved like the sea with its empty tides. Waiting, the wolves returned to the place where Feronia had disappeared. One full moon sank into the dark sky, then another and then another.

Devana watched the moon blossom and fade for countless cycles. Devastated by loneliness and grief, she called for a ceremony where she could speak with the spirit gods themselves.

Dressed in skins, Devana and her consorts hunted the deer. As the thick blood spilled, Devana, dancing in a frenzied ritual, covered herself with the liquid heat. She called to the gods for guidance and swore that she would find Feronia.

The moon, sealing itself into the black sky, watched cautiously as Devana began her search. Night after night, on the edge of the ridge, Devana called out into the abyss. Crying into the hollow wind, she wove hallucinations into visions; knitted visions into fragmented dreams. Over and over, the moon rose and fell like the sea. Devana, on the edge of the world, waited.

And tonight, the long waiting had passed.

Tonight it is the deer. Tonight it is the blood.

Chapter 16

Devana, her eyes alert, led the pack down the gradual slopes of the mountain. Moving to an overhang, she peered into the dark valley and howled. The others, who had separated and disappeared among the trees, echoed her call.

Feronia kept pace at Devana's side. Although she had proven her status in the pack, the dark wolf she had fought shadowed her every move. Following from a distance, the wolf lingered on the outside of the pack, always watching Feronia.

Feronia peered back at the wolf whose menacing teeth had come unnecessarily close to slicing her neck during the challenge. Feronia did not trust this wolf, whose power-hungry eyes pierced the night.

She moved next to Devana, on the cliff's edge, and let out a long howl. Glancing over her shoulder, she saw the dark wolf disappear into the trees.

"Did she run at your side while I was gone?" Feronia asked.

"Behind me a few paces, but never at my side." Devana stared ahead to the immense night sky.

"And if I hadn't returned?"

"But you have," Devana said emphatically. "And do not forget those who ran at *your* side while you were away."

Feronia was silent. She had forgotten — how quickly she had forgotten — those who had been at her side. She tried to envision them but could not draw forth their images. A sensation passed through her, not unlike an angry buzzing, then disappeared.

"But *that* is behind us, is it not, Feronia?" Devana was quick with her words. "As is Lupina, who has taken her rightful place in the pack."

Devana turned from the cliff and moved down the path. The others came from the trees to form the pack behind her. Preparing to continue their descent into the valley, Devana called to Feronia. But Feronia was motionless, fixed with a sudden uneasy feeling. She stared at Devana, encircled by the pack. They were restless in anticipation of the forthcoming sacrifice.

Feronia let out a single howl and the wolves called back in haunting harmonies. Her life, her place at Devana's side, awaited her. With the final spill of blood, the entire forest would bear witness to her homecoming.

She hurried to Devana's side and the pack continued toward the valley, all except Lupina who already was finding her own way through the trees.

Chapter 17

Behind me. Never at my side! The empty words ricocheted through Lupina's mind as she raced down the worn paths. As if Lupina had been a mere shadow and nothing more, Devana had effortlessly cast her aside.

How conveniently Devana had sidestepped any mention of her wildfire runs with Lupina. Never at her side, Lupina smirked as fiery flashbacks consumed her. They had run, side by side, oh how they had run. Egg-shaped pods, filled and weighted with Devana's mysterious magic, inserted deep in their cunts.

"Our secret," Devana, pleasure-master, had whispered.

She had pushed two smooth capsules, large as owl's eggs, into Lupina's slippery sex-pocket. "Now run!" The flickering gleam in Devana's eyes was always flagrantly apparent.

Devana raced with Lupina along hidden paths and rugged terrain. Deeply implanted, the spheres hit vigorously against each other. Every step brought quickening pleasure to Lupina. Like fast-moving snakes, sensations uncoiled. Tiny tongues lashed and vibrated in her womb.

"When you run at my side," Devana panted, well aware of the incredible passion the egg-pods produced, "there is always magic. I promise you that."

Against the wind, against the night, they pushed. Lupina's cunt walls quivered and clutched madly at the vibrating capsules. The pods knocked and Lupina's vagina sucked down tight.

Lupina concentrated as her inner muscles shuddered and pulsated involuntarily. The fluttering was good, sweet, like nothing she had ever experienced before her runs with Devana.

Devana nipped and snapped as she lunged onto Lupina. In wild embrace, they rolled down a grassy embankment, the eggs whacking intensely all the way.

"Devana!" Lupina screamed, ravaged by sex-pleasure. The pods slid up and down in her slippery, secret crevice.

"At my side, there is always magic," Devana had repeated again and again.

Into the field, into the high grass, they had tumbled. Lupina above Devana, then below. Above then below. Face in the flowers, ass on the ground, rolling over and over as the heavy pods snapped.

Devana turned Lupina onto her stomach and forced her ass to the sky. Lupina moaned in anticipation. It was always different, it was always the same, with Devana. Devana — strong and determined — above her. Legs intertwined, Devana jerked Lupina back and forth. The eggs smacked deliciously as Devana creased her fingers, one then two, into Lupina's tender ass-slit.

Devana applied pressure to the smooth skin-floor of the seldom trespassed canal, pushing the vaginal ceiling low. Back and forth, back and forth, as Devana pressed and tapped the hardened, smooth tunnel floor, the vaginal ceiling massaged the gyrating balls.

Lupina glided on Devana's knowing fingers. In and out, Devana's fingers tapped, tapped, tapped, until Lupina crashed into a convoluting wave of release.

"You like running at my side, don't you, Lupina?" Devana had whispered.

"Never at her side!" Lupina snapped angrily as she hurried down the mountain, enraged. The harsh memories were dark and brittle as the night air.

Feronia had come home, and everyone expected Lupina to blend into the pack. As if her time at Devana's side were nothing to consider, as if Feronia would replace Lupina and all would be forgotten. But Lupina had ideas of her own.

There were weaknesses, Lupina thought cunningly, unstable fissures that Devana, in her eagerness, was not attending to. In Feronia's extended time away, certain foundations had been laid, ties with the other world must have been established. And what? Did Devana think those recollections would evaporate like summer rain? Perhaps so, but Lupina knew better. Sweet memories, like mountain streams, ran deep. But eventually, they would surface.

Lupina, increasing her pace, darted down a steep path toward the mountain's base. She recalled Devana's words to Feronia: *Do not forget those who ran at your side while you were away.* Somewhere, down in the clearing, was where Feronia had returned. It was this place, Lupina was certain, where the stream of Feronia's memories would surface onto very fertile grounds.

Hadn't Devana spoken of another one from the vision-world stumbling about in the meadow? Was there not someone from Feronia's other world still searching for her, as Devana once had? If confronted with her other-world companion, would not Feronia's memory be jolted?

Lupina must discover Feronia's companion before Devana had a chance to destroy her. She'd find the consort, and then, in a masterful coup de grace, rekindle Feronia's memories. In a stunning moment of weakness, faced by her other lover, Feronia would become uncertain. Let Devana see Feronia's uncertainty! Let Devana be faced with her blatant betrayal!

Soon enough, Lupina would reclaim her rightful place at Devana's side, once and for all.

* * * * *

Reaching the base of the mountain, Lupina slowed her pace. It was somewhere in the meadow, not far beyond, that Devana had first come upon Feronia.

Lupina paused, her ears pricked. A stirring sound, quite close, caught her attention. Snout in the air, she attuned herself to the forest scents. A jackrabbit, on the left, munched quietly. A raccoon in the brush ahead stood frozen. Concealed in the shadows, Lupina softly crept to where another sweet scent, the most sacred of scents, emanated.

On the other side of the trees stood an exquisite deer. Lupina stiffened, not wanting to alert the deer to her presence.

The deer, not moving, seemed oblivious to its surroundings. She was staring ahead, into the night, as though lost in thought.

Lupina's entire body crackled with anticipation. What if she were to take this deer, have it down, sprawled in a pool of sacred blood when the others arrived in the meadow. Would they ignore her then? She took a step toward the deer and a twig broke underfoot.

Hearing the noise, the deer turned and called in the night. "Veronica? Is that you, Veronica?"

Lupina hesitated, astonished. She had expected the deer to race for the safety of the brush. What kind of deer would stand in the face of danger, unafraid?

"It's me. Amanda," the deer said, her voice smooth. "I have transformed into a deer. I've come to take you home."

Lupina tried to contain the immense exhilaration sweeping through her. Standing among the trees, in the guise of a gentle deer, was the very thing that would bring Feronia's magnificent downfall.

"It is not Veronica you have found," Lupina whispered breathlessly. The words swirled through the night air. "But I can take you to her."

"Who are you? I can't see you," the deer said cautiously.

Lupina moved out into the open. "I can take you to her," she repeated as she crossed in front of the deer. She bared her teeth as she spoke. "But you will have to trust me."

The vulnerable deer did not move. Instead, standing determined, she stared directly into Lupina's eyes.

Chapter 18

Nose to the ground, Lupina moved swiftly. Amanda followed close behind. Through the brush they traveled on the worn path, sometimes twisting up the base of the mountain then back down to the level ground.

At long last, she was on her way, Amanda thought, filled with relief. And the wolf, a most precarious guide on which to rely, seemed determined in her movements. It was as if the wolf had as much to gain as Amanda.

Amanda's breath was shallow from the run. Her

heart thumped relentlessly in her chest. She was tired yet filled with unleashed power. She could run forever to Veronica, her lovely Veronica.

The wolf abruptly raced around a tree. Looping back to Amanda, the wolf halted in front of her.

"This is where we wait," the wolf said. She glanced to the canyon that spread before them like a dark, thick quilt.

"Will you tell me now — now that we are taking a moment to rest — about Veronica?" Amanda said, her voice still uneven from the run. "Is she held against her will? Is she okay?"

"She is disoriented," said Lupina, "and may have no memory of you."

There was a faint howling from the mountains. Lupina moved closer to the periphery of the vast valley, her ears pointed and alert.

"They are closer and will enter the meadow soon. They search for a sacrifice to honor *your* Victoria's forthcoming allegiance to their clan."

Lupina paused, then stepped close to Amanda. "This is your last chance, your only hope. As the wolves reach the border of this meadow, you must be waiting for them in the center as though you were simply grazing. They will watch you from every angle. You must wait for them to make their move. And they will want you, oh sweet Amanda, how they will thirst for you!

"Making a circle, on the outskirts of the meadow, they will surround you. From all around, they will step from the darkness and begin their rush with a silent breath. The only way you will be certain that it has begun is when you see them, like deadly shadows, racing from the trees. It is then that you must scream, from the depths of your soul, for Veronica. Scream, and pray to the gods, that you wake her from her trance."

Amanda walked over to the edge of the brush and peered to the desolate clearing. "And if I fail?" she asked solemnly.

"If you fail," Lupina replied darkly, "then I will have no choice but to take you down myself."

The Shattering

Chapter 19

"Amanda!"

Eyes wide with terror, Jason bolted forward in bed. He had seen a vision of Amanda against the hard ground, her blood splattered everywhere. Somehow he had lost her. He had been cold and she had gone for shelter . . . and then . . . and then?

Jason swung his legs over the side of the bed. A sharp pain, thin and fierce as a stiletto, plunged deep into his brain.

"Jesus Christ," he cried as he fell back onto the bed. Stunned by the throbbing, unable to move, he clutched his head. Voices, seductively alluring, whispered to him from the darkness.

Go home, Jason. You're not needed here, Jason.

Occasional hallucinations, darting like sparrows, fluttered before his closed eyes — he was climbing a steep hill with a large rifle swung over his shoulder.

He lay like that, for how long he was uncertain, waiting, praying for the piercing pain to subside. At long last, he escaped into anesthetizing sleep.

Jason was tired. He had been climbing uphill for a considerable time. Veronica was lost, Amanda was missing, and he was uncertain of where he was headed.

Following a path through the trees, he stumbled over an occasional rock. He had only the light of the moon, his compass and the call of the wolves to guide him.

The rifle, tucked haphazardly under his arm, was bulky and uncomfortable, yet he was certain that he would be needing it. He was on a mission to rescue Veronica, and God only knew what dangers lurked in the shadows of this nightmare.

And where the hell had Amanda vanished to, he thought, filling with rage. Perhaps she had already found Veronica. Perhaps she had even taken Veronica from the dream without mentioning Jason — no reason for her to allude to Jason — leaving him a prisoner in this dark dream.

"Damn bitch!" Jason muttered as he kicked at a large rock. The rock, firmly embedded in the ground, did not budge. Instead, Jason tumbled and the rifle smashed hard against the ground in front of him.

With a loud explosion, the rifle discharged, sending a deafening boom throughout the forest. The stillness around him immediately broke into a deluge of scurrying sounds.

He suddenly felt vulnerable. Until this moment, he had assumed that he was alone. He had not considered the creatures hidden in the brush who blended with the night. Had they been watching him? Was every move he made somehow being relayed back to the horsewoman who had stolen his Veronica?

"Who's out there?" Jason called.

Aiming toward the sky, he fired another shot, then another, into the blackness. Reloading, he blitzed the night with a barrage of gunfire as if this act alone would somehow establish his position, his power.

Oh yes, *he* had the gun, Jason thought with a smirk. *He* had the final weapon to blast this damn dream into fragments. He was on his way, was closing in. The gun blasts made that fact perfectly clear.

"Do you hear that?" he screamed defiantly. "I'm coming for you, Veronica!"

The forest had become silent. All of the small creatures had taken cover and were still as the night. The scent of danger was strong and the gunfire thunderous. The creatures knew all too well to hide . . . and wait. There was one thing, and one thing only, that could protect them from this terrifying intruder.

Although unnoticed by the overconfident hunter, the padded footsteps of the approaching wolf, racing through the woods, was well heeded by the others.

The bombardment of gunfire shattering the forest caused Devana to stop dead in her tracks. Who could have penetrated the forest in such a way? Who had access to the weapon of the hunter?

Certainly not the woman, Amanda — Devana had taken care of *that* situation with a stunning stroke of genius. Wearing the cloak of the butterfly, she had spun an intoxicating cocoon around Amanda, convincing her to become a deer.

How Devana had relished the image of her upcoming final victory! In a remarkable coup, an unaware Feronia herself would bring forth that first spill of blood.

Confident that she had solved the problem of Amanda, caught up in Feronia's homecoming, Devana lost sight of everything else. Her guard down, Devana had spent her energy dancing amid the trees, parading her position, attempting to impress Feronia in every way possible. She had not been cautious, had no longer paid attention to the rest of the forest until this very moment.

And now, an unanticipated twist was at hand. That gun blast, from somewhere down the mountain, had awoken her from her euphoria. Rambling about in the forest, armed and dangerous, was the consequence of her reckless folly.

"Althea!" Devana called, a distinctive edge in her voice.

"Yes, Devana." Althea came from the trees, her eyes flame-red.

"Go ahead. Find who treads with such weapons in our forest." Devana was whispering, carefully guarding each word.

"And then?" Althea hissed, her sharp teeth white in the moon's filtered light.

"Return to me with your findings." Devana shot a glance at Feronia, who stood near a large rock with a look of concern on her face. "I will make my decision then."

Nodding, Althea melted into the shadows.

Feronia watched Althea disappear and then approached Devana. "Are there hunters?"

Devana turned to Feronia. "Not for long," she growled. For indeed, there was nothing that would ever take her Feronia away from her side again. Nothing!

Althea sprinted noiselessly from the trees. Her body was tense, as if she had seen something unexpected. Panting, barely able to speak, she reached the ridge where Devana and the others were waiting.

Devana could sense Althea's alarm the minute their eyes made contact. Swiftly she moved to Althea, leading her to the shadows.

"There is more, much more than we've anticipated" Althea spoke rapidly, her words staccato.

"The one with the berries, he has returned?" Devana's voice was calm. "I had thought as much. Of course he would return, looking for her."

"Devana," Althea said, moving even closer. "It is more than that. Yes, he has returned but —"

"He will no longer be a problem, now that I am aware of what is before me. I had lost myself and become careless, until now." Devana shook her head. An air of confidence cloaked her. "I will spin a vision around him. Before long he won't —"

"Our problem is Lupina," Althea said sharply, interrupting Devana.

"Lupina?" Devana said, caught unaware. She shot a quick glance to the others. Lupina was not among them.

"I had seen the man with the weapon. I knew who he was, that we could take care of him easily," Althea continued, her voice tight with tension. "On my return, I cut across the grade to scout the meadow. It is there that I saw them, in the trees. They were talking — Lupina and the deer."

"Lupina and the deer?" Devana said fiercely, her eyes cutting back to Althea. "Lupina and the deer, *talking*?"

"I believe Lupina has betrayed us, has betrayed you, Devana."

Devana stared mutely ahead. What could Lupina have revealed to the woman? Images raced before her eyes: Feronia entering the meadow, the deer standing, waiting, prepared to awaken unwelcomed memories —

"I must stop her!" Devana's voice was trembling. "We are at the turning point, Althea. After this moon is veiled and twilight is upon us, the passageway will once again be lost to us." Devana crossed in front of Althea and stared into her eyes. "One miscalculation and I lose Feronia."

"Do we retreat until the moon is shadowed?" Althea asked in a whisper.

"And sit idly as the trespassers are enclosed in our world? Enemies, forever pursuing us?" Devana snapped. "Surely you are not thinking clearly, Althea!"

"We could take them down, all of them."

"And tell Feronia what?" Devana began to pace. "Tell her that we killed her consorts? Tell her what, Althea? What would we say that would keep her heart from pulling away in grief?"

Taking a moment to gather her thoughts, Devana took a few steps further into the darkness.

"We will wait until that very last moment. The moon will be slipping from the sky, the sun's purpose not yet clearly defined. There will be only seconds. The passage between our two worlds will be narrowing." Devana's voice was trance-like. "We will need the herbs and leaves. Find them and come back to me."

Althea nodded and hurried into the forest. Devana gazed into the circle of wolves who were waiting patiently for her, her beloved Feronia among them.

"Everything in my power," Devana — dream artist, spinner of silk illusions — murmured as she returned to her sweet Feronia's side.

Chapter 20

"Who in the name of the Goddess is that?" Lupina said, startled. The forest was suddenly quiet again. The blast of gunfire had ceased.

"Jason!" Amanda said quickly. "He has found his way!"

"With a weapon?" Lupina's ears were perked to the sound. She listened for the intruder. "He has no idea what he is walking into. He could destroy us all."

"Should I try to find him and alert him to our plan?" Amanda asked. She glanced toward the meadow and wondered how much time she had before the wolves arrived.

"There is not enough time," Lupina said, anger coloring her words. Rage boiled within her. Things were becoming more and more complicated. Her life had been thrown into turmoil because of Feronia. And where was Devana through all of this? How easily Devana had forsaken and abandoned her.

Fragmented memories sliced into Lupina like slivers of glass. Who had sat with Devana all those lonely nights? Lupina thought recklessly. Who had listened to Devana? And the long hours, the moonless nights, the never-ending months Lupina had slept at Devana's side! Did that not account for anything? Devana had not even glanced toward Lupina since Feronia's return.

Lupina let out a low growl. "We will continue as we have planned."

And if the hunter took them all down, Lupina deliberated, so it would be. For what did she have to look forward to, now that she had a moment to see things clearly? Amanda would call out to Feronia and a flash-flood of memories would overwhelm Feronia. There would be a split-second when Feronia would have to choose between Devana and Amanda, for once Amanda was recognized, Devana would demand that someone, anyone, kill the deer immediately. Feronia would either attempt to protect Amanda or watch helplessly as she was torn to shreds.

If Feronia did not escape the other world with Amanda, how could Feronia ever forgive Devana for Amanda's brutal death? It would always seep between them like a rotting disease. Which is exactly what Lupina had originally hoped for. She had fantasized comforting a brokenhearted Devana once again.

And yet, Lupina wondered if she could ever forgive Devana for the coldness, the abrupt desertion. Would the outcome in the meadow even matter? Let the hunter take them all, Lupina thought, defeated. In reality, there was nothing left for her anyway.

"I only spent a short time with Veronica." Amanda's words broke Lupina's thoughts. They walked toward the center of the meadow, side by side. "And yet there was a quality about her that made me fall in love immediately. I was swept away by her."

"I've never been loved like that," Lupina answered, overcome with emptiness.

She had chosen to accompany Amanda into the field, but was unsure why. Perhaps it was the complete sadness she felt. The realization that her relationship with Devana was hopeless had hit her hard. As Amanda spoke about her love for Feronia, Lupina wished someone would love her in that same all-consuming way.

"And after we made love," Amanda said softly, "the bond between us intensified. Veronica didn't want to go home. She wanted to stay with me. Can you imagine? One weekend and she had found more than in all the years she spent with Jason."

"I had thought you'd been together for a long time." Lupina turned to face Amanda and was struck by the warmth, the depth of love, in the deer's eyes.

Amanda reached the center of the meadow and stared at the setting moon. "A long time? And what is time when it comes to love?"

Lupina said nothing. In the quiet, she could sense the wolves. She was certain that Devana and the others had reached the border of the clearing.

The Passageway

Chapter 21

As they reached the perimeter of the meadow, Devana shot a quick glance to Althea. It was just as she had said. Lupina and the deer were together. They stood, the most unlikely of companions, in the center of the field.

It was almost daybreak. There was not much time. It would be up to Devana to make the move, to enter into the field, to spill the blood.

Silently, she stepped out of the shadows. The vivid taste of the leaves Althea had collected caused her saliva to flow freely. She had the special herbs tucked between her teeth and cheek. She was ready. There would be one chance and one chance only.

Jason reached the edge of the field. It was just as he was told it would be. The deer and the wolf were waiting for him. After all he had been through, he would finally take her home.

After the gunfire, after Jason's show of strength, the most exquisite butterfly had appeared.

"I have chosen you to save her," the butterfly, symbol of hope, had said flirtatiously.

Enraptured, Jason watched the butterfly. With a dancer's grace, she slowly opened her diamond-beaded wings and a flurry of shimmering colors swirled around him.

"With your power and your obvious strengths . . ." The butterfly closed her hooded eyes to alluring half-slits and slipped her pink tongue between her nectar-wet lips. ". . . you alone can bring her home. But you must hurry, for time is running short."

She encircled him in her jewel-spun wings and a waterfall of glitter cascaded over him. Her flowery scent enchanted him. Her seductive whispering bewitched him.

"First you must . . ." The butterfly had instructed him as they hurried through the night. "And then you must . . ." Had they soared in the air? Had they run along the worn paths? One moment in the forest, the next he was alone at the meadow's edge.

The night was breaking into yellows and pinks. Just as the butterfly had promised, the deer and the wolf stood in the field. The time had come to take his Veronica home.

Devana opened into a fast trot, moving in on the wolf and the deer. Off to the side, she could see the hunter as he broke into a run.

"Veronica! Veronica!" Amanda yelled at the approaching wolf. Its teeth were bared and saliva flowed profusely from its mouth. "It's me. I have come back for you!"

The wolf did not stop; in fact, it increased its hungry pace. The scent of destruction enveloped them all.

Lupina was in awe. This was not what she had anticipated. Devana, alone, was heading toward them, an evil yellow haze in her eyes.

"Devana, no!" Lupina cried.

The sound of gunfire shattered the air. Jason was shooting haphazardly into the sky, apparently unable to decipher Veronica from the enemy.

"No," he screamed helplessly. "Veronica? Veronica!"

Devana lunged through the air like a black spear ready to make its mark. She leaped, pouncing on Lupina who slammed against the ground with a hard thud.

Devana's sharp teeth sliced into Lupina's throat. She growled deeply as her herb-tainted saliva mixed with Lupina's blood.

"No!" Jason screamed. He crashed on top of them and unsuccessfully tried to pull them apart.

The sun was slicing through the dark, the light seeped in. Her mission completed, Devana hurried into the trees, the taste of Lupina's blood fresh in her mouth.

The hunter wept as he clung to the bleeding wolf. The deer stood, stunned, staring after Devana. "Veronica? Veronica?" she cried desperately.

Althea, followed by six others, rushed into the field. In a ritual run, they encircled the crying hunter, the screaming deer and the listless wolf. The sun broke the sky and the passageway closed.

Sunrise had cut night and the pregnant sun rose in the sky. Devana studied the wolves that had reunited with her partway up the hill.

"We will explain our loss as an accident. The weapon, the gunfire, it will be easily believed."

The others were quiet as Devana spoke. Her voice was steady yet tense with unleashed power. They understood what was required for their own good, for the good of the entire pack.

"Then it is done," Devana said, her eyes darted to each wolf, each separate set of eyes.

Yes, it is done, Althea thought.

Devana and Althea began the ascent up the hill with the others following. The remainder of the pack was waiting for them, having spent the night near a small cave not too far up the mountain.

Amanda:
The Awakening

Chapter 22

I opened my eyes. We were in bed, clinging to each other. Jason was especially restless. He tossed in his sleep, mumbling incoherently.

"Veronica," I said softly. I ran my fingertip across her brow.

Asleep, Veronica looked remarkably content, as though she had simply had a full night's rest and nothing more.

"Veronica?" I whispered again. God, how I had missed her! I wanted to wake her, to steal her away before Jason woke and started with his inevitable tantrum.

Veronica stirred slightly. I traced my fingertip across her lips and she moved again. Her eyes opened and I stared into them. I felt more entranced than ever.

"Amanda? Amanda!" she said with an excitement, almost an exhilaration, surging in her voice.

"You are home," I whispered. I pointed to Jason. "We're not ready to wake him, are we?"

She shook her head with a smile. More beautiful than I had remembered, Veronica's eyes had a new sparkle, a glow I hadn't noticed before.

"It is you, it is you, it is you!" Veronica chanted in a joyous half-whisper.

She climbed out of bed, stretched and danced around the room. "You and me, Amanda. Am I right? You'll love me forever, Amanda?"

"Forever," I said as I took her in my arms. "Forever and ever."

We hurried outside and walked in the morning air. Veronica was exuberant. She delighted in the sound of the bobwhites, the heat of the sun, the scent of lavender and lilac. It was as if her journey had rejuvenated her, giving her a new appreciation of life.

"There is no way I'll go back to him," she said as she danced ahead of me. She crossed the gravel road to the flower-laden field. "I feel a sense of freedom like I've never felt before. All because of you, Amanda!"

"While you were in the dream, did you ever think that you wanted to stay with them? Live that life?" I asked hesitantly.

"The time I spent there was long enough," Veronica said. She picked a daisy and handed it to me. "The love that you have for me is all I want. I never want to leave you again — not for the dreams, not for Jason."

"No more dream trips, huh, Miss I-have-to-go-back," I said with a laugh. I grabbed her, pressing her soft body against mine as we tumbled into the flowers.

I kissed her full lips, her smooth cheeks, her silky eyelids. I was lost in the scent of her — or was it the lavender, was it the buttercups?

She lifted my skirt. My nipples tightened in anticipation of her touch. Veronica had a new certainty about her, about us. She touched me as if she had made love to women countless times before — which was fine, I wanted to be taken. I needed to feel the assurance of her desire for me.

She pressed her hands against my belly then pushed slowly to my breasts. Her hands roughly caressed my nipples, then gave an aggressive tug.

"I will keep you happy," she muttered. "Happier than you can ever imagine."

My nipples stung from the pressure of her pinch. Waves of excitement shot through me.

"Oh yes," I moaned.

"Just promise that you'll love me with all your heart," she coaxed, guiding me onto my stomach.

"Yes," I promised. "All my heart."

My face pressed into the flowered grass. Smothered in lavender and buttercups, surrounded by honeysuckle and lilacs, I was in a bed of spun flowers.

Veronica quickly tugged off her clothes then pulled down my pants. As she straddled my ass, I felt the softness of her sweet, velvet pussy. Her fleshy breasts flattened against my back, her soft thighs grabbed my full hips.

"Like it wild?" she teased in my ear as she nipped lightly on my neck.

She tangled her fingers in my hair and jerked my head. Her pussy, flush against my ass, was sopping and her sticky lips seemed to grasp my skin. Sliding across one cheek then the next, she dragged her thickened pussy-flesh across me. Her clit seemed extraordinarily extended. I could envision the enlarged vulva, thick and plush, hanging low from her body.

I had to see, I needed to see. I pushed, struggled, I rolled myself onto my back. As I had imagined — and how delicious, how erotic — her tuft of flesh was bulbously suspended, the color magnificently flushed. What an entrancing contrast to her dark-haired lips!

As though answering my hopes, Veronica straddled my face and dangled her scarlet package only inches from my tongue. Slowly teasing the elongated little lips against my nose and eyes, she made me crazy with excitement.

I grabbed her hips — I had to taste her. I pulled her down — I had to smell her, suck her, lap her, plunge into her slippery slit. My face was submerged in purple-pink pillows and soaking wet velvets.

Veronica began to jerk wildly, riding my face. This was a new Veronica, a different Veronica than

I had experienced. She was like the jungle, untamed and out of control.

Up and down, she fucked my tongue with her hardened pussy. Each time she lifted, each time she came down, I crammed my pointed tongue against the raised rim of her opening. She squeezed down, she tightened her muscles, she sucked at my mouth with her quivering sex-lips.

In a grinding motion, her flapping pussy rotated against me. Her hips thrust as she bucked against my face. Her clit was fat. The red flush had swelled into a deep purple-blue. I'd never seen a woman so enlarged, so remarkably swollen. Her flesh dangled and teased, rubbed and slid. I was drenched in her juices, smothered in the soft-hardness of her pussy. She was spongy yet rigid, slippery yet sticky. Salty, sweet, flaccid, taut.

I grabbed her lips and stretched her apart. Her clit jutted from the plump, red, pillowy encasement. I sucked, oh yes, sucked and sucked that little button between my lips. Faster and faster, her cunt on my face. Wet reds, dark reds, slippery, sliding, electric reds.

I slipped a finger in. The creaming passage tightened hungrily on my twisting finger. I slipped in another. Veronica clamped hard. Her inner walls were firm and unyielding.

"So you *do* like it wild," Veronica said, her voice steamy.

She pulled away from my face, slid from my fingers in an abrupt movement.

"C'mon," she growled as she yanked me from the ground. "I'll show you wild."

With little shoves she pushed me, coercing me to move backwards.

"Veronica," I giggled, impressed with her aggressiveness.

Her eyes filled with unguarded passion, her mouth set with uncompromising desire, she shoved again. Three steps back. She pushed again. Two steps back. Again. The rough bark of an oak tree scratched into me as she pressed me back one final step.

"You see," she mumbled as she reached for a thick rope that hung from a low branch, "I like it wild, too."

Veronica's sultry words stormed though me as she skimmed the coarse hemp cord back and forth across the sensitive skin of my stomach.

"You like it?" she asked, her voice sensuous, her words syrupy.

Her eyes greedily scanned my breasts. She rolled the rope from my belly to my flushed nipples. The fibers roughly grazed against the pert nuggets. Over and over, she slid the rope. The nipples were soon chafed and pepper-red.

"And then, and then . . ." she muttered as she forced my legs apart with her knee.

She swiftly tied the rope, repeatedly, until it was bunched like an uneven, gnarled ball. She tied the loose ends of the rope behind her back so the tangled, bulky center knot pressed against her thick mound.

Veronica pushed into me and the knotted rope pressed against my lips.

"Spread them," she demanded.

Spread my legs? My pussy? Naked against the tree, Veronica and I were locked in a fervid embrace. Whatever she wanted, she could have. I spread my legs, I pulled my pussy apart.

With a movement slow and precise, Veronica eased the bulky material between my stretched lips. She lightly pressed, just enough for the hard fibers to gently scrape my clitoris. No more.

"I will treat you like no other." Her breath was hot in my ear. "I will comfort you, pamper you, sleep at your side."

The coarse knot barely grazed my distended vulva.

"Just promise me, promise me, you'll . . ." Veronica's words were muffled as she pushed against me.

The bark scraped into my back, her fingers held my hair, her nails cut into my arm. The thick knot edged against my fleshy clit, just enough to flatten it. I tensed, anticipating the unknown sensation one hard thrust would produce. Instead, with an exact tension, Veronica stopped. Her lack of movement, merged with her controlled, tightened trembling, caused the rough fibers to unmercifully tease my throbbing, puckered flesh.

I grabbed her ass. I slammed her hips against mine. Would it hurt? I didn't care. The knot cleaved my lips, scratched against my swollen flesh. Veronica held steady. She didn't move. The pressure of the rope, her wild scent, the heat from the morning sun . . . I rotated my hips; hot pleasure heaved through me.

"Always at my side," she mumbled.

Veronica's body was tense from lack of movement. She stared into my eyes as though branding her words in my memory.

"Say it," she demanded. Her body trembled. Her glaring eyes penetrated.

"Always at your side," I whispered in a breath of rushed air that sliced the sudden silence.

With her eyes mysteriously alive, her mouth breaking into a flagrant smile, Veronica pushed into me. The husky, hard knot scraped my sex-flush. The sensation elicited both pleasure and pain — like a sharp bite, like digging fingernails, like a hard smack on the ass.

I cried out in pleasure-pain and we tumbled to the ground, rolling, the knot crammed in my pussy folds, her mouth wild on mine. The rough pleasure pierced my cunt. And we rolled in daisies, tumbled in violets, over and over, in a sea of purple passion, my Veronica and I.

Veronica:
Dream Reveler

Chapter 23

This is what I have deserved. This is what I have deserved from the very start, she thought, wrapped in Amanda's arms. In the field, the pleasure of lovemaking still fresh on them both, she dreamily gazed past the flowers, past the distant houses, to the thick trees. A woman like Amanda will love me forever. Devana hadn't really cared, not like this, not like Amanda.

Devana, dream-spinner, had tried to control destiny — mixing the sacred herbs as if she could trap Lupina, against her will, in the other world! As if she could force Lupina to take Veronica's place! But Lupina was no fool, not then, not now. Once she had understood, once the dizziness had begun, she had not resisted.

And here she now sat, a most enthusiastic pawn — the undisputed winner as far as she was concerned — of Devana's intricate game.

Lupina picked a daisy, pulling the petals one at a time.

"Loves me, loves me not?" Amanda, her face still flushed from orgasm, whispered.

Sprinkling the white petals in the air like a flurry of soft snowflakes, Lupina then kissed Amanda lightly on the lips.

"Loves me," she laughed. "Loves me, loves me, loves me."

A few of the publications of
THE NAIAD PRESS, INC.
P.O. Box 10543 • Tallahassee, Florida 32302
Phone (904) 539-5965
Toll-Free Order Number: 1-800-533-1973
Mail orders welcome. Please include 15% postage.
Write or call for our free catalog which also features an
incredible selection of lesbian videos.

COSTA BRAVA by Marta Balletbo Coll. 144 pp. Read the book,
see the movie!   ISBN 1-56280-153-8 $11.95

MEETING MAGDALENE & OTHER STORIES by
Marilyn Freeman. 160 pp. Read the book, see the movie!
                                             ISBN 1-56280-170-8   11.95

SECOND FIDDLE by Kate Calloway. 240 pp. P.I. Cassidy James'
second case.   ISBN 1-56280-169-6   11.95

LAUREL by Isabel Miller. 128 pp. By the author of the beloved
Patience and Sarah.   ISBN 1-56280-146-5   10.95

LOVE OR MONEY by Jackie Calhoun. 240 pp. The romance of
real life.   ISBN 1-56280-147-3   10.95

SMOKE AND MIRRORS by Pat Welch. 224 pp. 5th Helen Black
Mystery.   ISBN 1-56280-143-0   10.95

DANCING IN THE DARK edited by Barbara Grier & Christine
Cassidy. 272 pp. Erotic love stories by Naiad Press authors.
                                             ISBN 1-56280-144-9   14.95

TIME AND TIME AGAIN by Catherine Ennis. 176 pp. Passionate
love affair.   ISBN 1-56280-145-7   10.95

PAXTON COURT by Diane Salvatore. 256 pp. Erotic and wickedly
funny contemporary tale about the business of learning to live
together.   ISBN 1-56280-114-7   10.95

INNER CIRCLE by Claire McNab. 208 pp. 8th Carol Ashton
Mystery.   ISBN 1-56280-135-X   10.95

LESBIAN SEX: AN ORAL HISTORY by Susan Johnson.
240 pp. Need we say more?   ISBN 1-56280-142-2   14.95

BABY, IT'S COLD by Jaye Maiman. 256 pp. 5th Robin Miller
Mystery.   ISBN 1-56280-141-4   19.95

WILD THINGS by Karin Kallmaker. 240 pp. By the undisputed
mistress of lesbian romance.   ISBN 1-56280-139-2   10.95

THE GIRL NEXT DOOR by Mindy Kaplan. 208 pp. Just what
you'd expect. ISBN 1-56280-140-6 10.95

NOW AND THEN by Penny Hayes. 240 pp. Romance on the
westward journey. ISBN 1-56280-121-X 10.95

HEART ON FIRE by Diana Simmonds. 176 pp. The romantic and
erotic rival of *Curious Wine.* ISBN 1-56280-152-X 10.95

DEATH AT LAVENDER BAY by Lauren Wright Douglas. 208 pp.
1st Allison O'Neil Mystery. ISBN 1-56280-085-X 10.95

YES I SAID YES I WILL by Judith McDaniel. 272 pp. Hot
romance by famous author. ISBN 1-56280-138-4 10.95

FORBIDDEN FIRES by Margaret C. Anderson. Edited by Mathilda
Hills. 176 pp. Famous author's "unpublished" Lesbian romance.
ISBN 1-56280-123-6 21.95

SIDE TRACKS by Teresa Stores. 160 pp. Gender-bending
Lesbians on the road. ISBN 1-56280-122-8 10.95

HOODED MURDER by Annette Van Dyke. 176 pp. 1st Jessie
Batelle Mystery. ISBN 1-56280-134-1 10.95

WILDWOOD FLOWERS by Julia Watts. 208 pp. Hilarious and
heart-warming tale of true love. ISBN 1-56280-127-9 10.95

NEVER SAY NEVER by Linda Hill. 224 pp. Rule #1: Never get involved
with . . . ISBN 1-56280-126-0 10.95

THE SEARCH by Melanie McAllester. 240 pp. Exciting top cop
Tenny Mendoza case. ISBN 1-56280-150-3 10.95

THE WISH LIST by Saxon Bennett. 192 pp. Romance through
the years. ISBN 1-56280-125-2 10.95

FIRST IMPRESSIONS by Kate Calloway. 208 pp. P.I. Cassidy
James' first case. ISBN 1-56280-133-3 10.95

OUT OF THE NIGHT by Kris Bruyer. 192 pp. Spine-tingling
thriller. ISBN 1-56280-120-1 10.95

NORTHERN BLUE by Tracey Richardson. 224 pp. Police recruits
Miki & Miranda — passion in the line of fire. ISBN 1-56280-118-X 10.95

LOVE'S HARVEST by Peggy J. Herring. 176 pp. by the author of
Once More With Feeling. ISBN 1-56280-117-1 10.95

THE COLOR OF WINTER by Lisa Shapiro. 208 pp. Romantic
love beyond your wildest dreams. ISBN 1-56280-116-3 10.95

FAMILY SECRETS by Laura DeHart Young. 208 pp. Enthralling
romance and suspense. ISBN 1-56280-119-8 10.95

INLAND PASSAGE by Jane Rule. 288 pp. Tales exploring conven-
tional & unconventional relationships. ISBN 0-930044-56-8 10.95

DOUBLE BLUFF by Claire McNab. 208 pp. 7th Carol Ashton
Mystery. ISBN 1-56280-096-5 10.95

BAR GIRLS by Lauran Hoffman. 176 pp. See the movie, read
the book! ISBN 1-56280-115-5 10.95

THE FIRST TIME EVER edited by Barbara Grier & Christine
Cassidy. 272 pp. Love stories by Naiad Press authors.
ISBN 1-56280-086-8 14.95

MISS PETTIBONE AND MISS McGRAW by Brenda Weathers.
208 pp. A charming ghostly love story. ISBN 1-56280-151-1 10.95

CHANGES by Jackie Calhoun. 208 pp. Involved romance and
relationships. ISBN 1-56280-083-3 10.95

FAIR PLAY by Rose Beecham. 256 pp. 3rd Amanda Valentine
Mystery. ISBN 1-56280-081-7 10.95

PAYBACK by Celia Cohen. 176 pp. A gripping thriller of romance,
revenge and betrayal. ISBN 1-56280-084-1 10.95

THE BEACH AFFAIR by Barbara Johnson. 224 pp. Sizzling
summer romance/mystery/intrigue. ISBN 1-56280-090-6 10.95

GETTING THERE by Robbi Sommers. 192 pp. Nobody does it
like Robbi! ISBN 1-56280-099-X 10.95

FINAL CUT by Lisa Haddock. 208 pp. 2nd Carmen Ramirez
Mystery. ISBN 1-56280-088-4 10.95

FLASHPOINT by Katherine V. Forrest. 256 pp. A Lesbian
blockbuster! ISBN 1-56280-079-5 10.95

CLAIRE OF THE MOON by Nicole Conn. Audio Book —Read
by Marianne Hyatt. ISBN 1-56280-113-9 16.95

FOR LOVE AND FOR LIFE: INTIMATE PORTRAITS OF
LESBIAN COUPLES by Susan Johnson. 224 pp.
ISBN 1-56280-091-4 14.95

DEVOTION by Mindy Kaplan. 192 pp. See the movie — read
the book! ISBN 1-56280-093-0 10.95

SOMEONE TO WATCH by Jaye Maiman. 272 pp. 4th Robin
Miller Mystery. ISBN 1-56280-095-7 10.95

GREENER THAN GRASS by Jennifer Fulton. 208 pp. A young
woman — a stranger in her bed. ISBN 1-56280-092-2 10.95

TRAVELS WITH DIANA HUNTER by Regine Sands. Erotic
lesbian romp. Audio Book (2 cassettes) ISBN 1-56280-107-4 16.95

CABIN FEVER by Carol Schmidt. 256 pp. Sizzling suspense
and passion. ISBN 1-56280-089-1 10.95

THERE WILL BE NO GOODBYES by Laura DeHart Young. 192
pp. Romantic love, strength, and friendship. ISBN 1-56280-103-1 10.95

FAULTLINE by Sheila Ortiz Taylor. 144 pp. Joyous comic
lesbian novel. ISBN 1-56280-108-2 9.95

OPEN HOUSE by Pat Welch. 176 pp. 4th Helen Black Mystery.
ISBN 1-56280-102-3 10.95

ONCE MORE WITH FEELING by Peggy J. Herring. 240 pp.
Lighthearted, loving romantic adventure.   ISBN 1-56280-089-2   10.95

FOREVER by Evelyn Kennedy. 224 pp. Passionate romance — love
overcoming all obstacles.   ISBN 1-56280-094-9   10.95

WHISPERS by Kris Bruyer. 176 pp. Romantic ghost story
     ISBN 1-56280-082-5   10.95

NIGHT SONGS by Penny Mickelbury. 224 pp. 2nd Gianna Maglione
Mystery.   ISBN 1-56280-097-3   10.95

GETTING TO THE POINT by Teresa Stores. 256 pp. Classic
southern Lesbian novel.   ISBN 1-56280-100-7   10.95

PAINTED MOON by Karin Kallmaker. 224 pp. Delicious
Kallmaker romance.   ISBN 1-56280-075-2   10.95

THE MYSTERIOUS NAIAD edited by Katherine V. Forrest &
Barbara Grier. 320 pp. Love stories by Naiad Press authors.
     ISBN 1-56280-074-4   14.95

DAUGHTERS OF A CORAL DAWN by Katherine V. Forrest.
240 pp. Tenth Anniversay Edition.   ISBN 1-56280-104-X   10.95

BODY GUARD by Claire McNab. 208 pp. 6th Carol Ashton
Mystery.   ISBN 1-56280-073-6   10.95

CACTUS LOVE by Lee Lynch. 192 pp. Stories by the beloved
storyteller.   ISBN 1-56280-071-X   9.95

SECOND GUESS by Rose Beecham. 216 pp. 2nd Amanda Valentine
Mystery.   ISBN 1-56280-069-8   9.95

A RAGE OF MAIDENS by Lauren Wright Douglas. 240 pp. 6th Caitlin
Reece Mystery.   ISBN 1-56280-068-X   10.95

TRIPLE EXPOSURE by Jackie Calhoun. 224 pp. Romantic drama
involving many characters.   ISBN 1-56280-067-1   10.95

UP, UP AND AWAY by Catherine Ennis. 192 pp. Delightful
romance.   ISBN 1-56280-065-5   9.95

PERSONAL ADS by Robbi Sommers. 176 pp. Sizzling short
stories.   ISBN 1-56280-059-0   10.95

CROSSWORDS by Penny Sumner. 256 pp. 2nd Victoria Cross
Mystery.   ISBN 1-56280-064-7   9.95

SWEET CHERRY WINE by Carol Schmidt. 224 pp. A novel of
suspense.   ISBN 1-56280-063-9   9.95

CERTAIN SMILES by Dorothy Tell. 160 pp. Erotic short stories.
     ISBN 1-56280-066-3   9.95

EDITED OUT by Lisa Haddock. 224 pp. 1st Carmen Ramirez
Mystery.   ISBN 1-56280-077-9   9.95

WEDNESDAY NIGHTS by Camarin Grae. 288 pp. Sexy
adventure.   ISBN 1-56280-060-4   10.95

SMOKEY O by Celia Cohen. 176 pp. Relationships on the
playing field.   ISBN 1-56280-057-4   9.95

KATHLEEN O'DONALD by Penny Hayes. 256 pp. Rose and
Kathleen find each other and employment in 1909 NYC.
                                                 ISBN 1-56280-070-1   9.95

STAYING HOME by Elisabeth Nonas. 256 pp. Molly and Alix
want a baby . . . or do they?   ISBN 1-56280-076-0   10.95

TRUE LOVE by Jennifer Fulton. 240 pp. Six lesbians searching
for love in all the "right" places.   ISBN 1-56280-035-3   10.95

KEEPING SECRETS by Penny Mickelbury. 208 pp. 1st Gianna
Maglione Mystery.   ISBN 1-56280-052-3   9.95

THE ROMANTIC NAIAD edited by Katherine V. Forrest &
Barbara Grier. 336 pp. Love stories by Naiad Press authors.
                                                 ISBN 1-56280-054-X   14.95

UNDER MY SKIN by Jaye Maiman. 336 pp. 3rd Robin Miller
Mystery.   ISBN 1-56280-049-3.   10.95

CAR POOL by Karin Kallmaker. 272pp. Lesbians on wheels
and then some!   ISBN 1-56280-048-5   10.95

NOT TELLING MOTHER: STORIES FROM A LIFE by Diane
Salvatore. 176 pp. Her 3rd novel.   ISBN 1-56280-044-2   9.95

GOBLIN MARKET by Lauren Wright Douglas. 240pp. 5th Caitlin
Reece Mystery.   ISBN 1-56280-047-7   10.95

LONG GOODBYES by Nikki Baker. 256 pp. 3rd Virginia Kelly
Mystery.   ISBN 1-56280-042-6   9.95

FRIENDS AND LOVERS by Jackie Calhoun. 224 pp. Mid-
western Lesbian lives and loves.   ISBN 1-56280-041-8   10.95

THE CAT CAME BACK by Hilary Mullins. 208 pp. Highly
praised Lesbian novel.   ISBN 1-56280-040-X   9.95

BEHIND CLOSED DOORS by Robbi Sommers. 192 pp. Hot,
erotic short stories.   ISBN 1-56280-039-6   9.95

CLAIRE OF THE MOON by Nicole Conn. 192 pp. See the
movie — read the book!   ISBN 1-56280-038-8   10.95

SILENT HEART by Claire McNab. 192 pp. Exotic Lesbian
romance.   ISBN 1-56280-036-1   10.95

THE SPY IN QUESTION by Amanda Kyle Williams. 256 pp.
4th Madison McGuire Mystery.   ISBN 1-56280-037-X   9.95

SAVING GRACE by Jennifer Fulton. 240 pp. Adventure and
romantic entanglement.   ISBN 1-56280-051-5   10.95

CURIOUS WINE by Katherine V. Forrest. 176 pp. Tenth Anniver-
sary Edition. The most popular contemporary Lesbian love story.
                                                 ISBN 1-56280-053-1   10.95
    Audio Book (2 cassettes)   ISBN 1-56280-105-8   16.95

CHAUTAUQUA by Catherine Ennis. 192 pp. Exciting, romantic
adventure.   ISBN 1-56280-032-9   9.95
A PROPER BURIAL by Pat Welch. 192 pp. 3rd Helen Black
Mystery.   ISBN 1-56280-033-7   9.95
SILVERLAKE HEAT: A Novel of Suspense by Carol Schmidt.
240 pp. Rhonda is as hot as Laney's dreams.   ISBN 1-56280-031-0   9.95
LOVE, ZENA BETH by Diane Salvatore. 224 pp. The most talked
about lesbian novel of the nineties!   ISBN 1-56280-030-2   10.95
A DOORYARD FULL OF FLOWERS by Isabel Miller. 160 pp.
Stories incl. 2 sequels to *Patience and Sarah.*   ISBN 1-56280-029-9   9.95
MURDER BY TRADITION by Katherine V. Forrest. 288 pp. 4th
Kate Delafield Mystery.   ISBN 1-56280-002-7   11.95
THE EROTIC NAIAD edited by Katherine V. Forrest & Barbara
Grier. 224 pp. Love stories by Naiad Press authors.
                                          ISBN 1-56280-026-4   14.95
DEAD CERTAIN by Claire McNab. 224 pp. 5th Carol Ashton
Mystery.   ISBN 1-56280-027-2   10.95
CRAZY FOR LOVING by Jaye Maiman. 320 pp. 2nd Robin Miller
Mystery.   ISBN 1-56280-025-6   10.95
STONEHURST by Barbara Johnson. 176 pp. Passionate regency
romance.   ISBN 1-56280-024-8   9.95
INTRODUCING AMANDA VALENTINE by Rose Beecham.
256 pp. 1st Amanda Valentine Mystery.   ISBN 1-56280-021-3   10.95
UNCERTAIN COMPANIONS by Robbi Sommers. 204 pp.
Steamy, erotic novel.   ISBN 1-56280-017-5   9.95
A TIGER'S HEART by Lauren W. Douglas. 240 pp. 4th Caitlin
Reece Mystery.   ISBN 1-56280-018-3   9.95
PAPERBACK ROMANCE by Karin Kallmaker. 256 pp. A
delicious romance.   ISBN 1-56280-019-1   10.95
THE LAVENDER HOUSE MURDER by Nikki Baker. 224 pp.
2nd Virginia Kelly Mystery.   ISBN 1-56280-012-4   9.95
PASSION BAY by Jennifer Fulton. 224 pp. Passionate romance,
virgin beaches, tropical skies.   ISBN 1-56280-028-0   10.95
STICKS AND STONES by Jackie Calhoun. 208 pp. Contemporary
lesbian lives and loves.   ISBN 1-56280-020-5   9.95
Audio Book (2 cassettes)   ISBN 1-56280-106-6   16.95
UNDER THE SOUTHERN CROSS by Claire McNab. 192 pp.
Romantic nights Down Under.   ISBN 1-56280-011-6   9.95
GRASSY FLATS by Penny Hayes. 256 pp. Lesbian romance in
the '30s.   ISBN 1-56280-010-8   9.95
A SINGULAR SPY by Amanda K. Williams. 192 pp. 3rd
Madison McGuire Mystery.   ISBN 1-56280-008-6   8.95

THE END OF APRIL by Penny Sumner. 240 pp. 1st Victoria
Cross Mystery.   ISBN 1-56280-007-8   8.95

KISS AND TELL by Robbi Sommers. 192 pp. Scorching stories
by the author of *Pleasures*.   ISBN 1-56280-005-1   10.95

STILL WATERS by Pat Welch. 208 pp. 2nd Helen Black Mystery.
                  ISBN 0-941483-97-5   9.95

TO LOVE AGAIN by Evelyn Kennedy. 208 pp. Wildly romantic
love story.   ISBN 0-941483-85-1   9.95

IN THE GAME by Nikki Baker. 192 pp. 1st Virginia Kelly
Mystery.   ISBN 1-56280-004-3   9.95

STRANDED by Camarin Grae. 320 pp. Entertaining, riveting
adventure.   ISBN 0-941483-99-1   9.95

THE DAUGHTERS OF ARTEMIS by Lauren Wright Douglas.
240 pp. 3rd Caitlin Reece Mystery.   ISBN 0-941483-95-9   9.95

CLEARWATER by Catherine Ennis. 176 pp. Romantic secrets
of a small Louisiana town.   ISBN 0-941483-65-7   8.95

THE HALLELUJAH MURDERS by Dorothy Tell. 176 pp. 2nd
Poppy Dillworth Mystery.   ISBN 0-941483-88-6   8.95

SECOND CHANCE by Jackie Calhoun. 256 pp. Contemporary
Lesbian lives and loves.   ISBN 0-941483-93-2   9.95

BENEDICTION by Diane Salvatore. 272 pp. Striking, contemporary romantic novel.   ISBN 0-941483-90-8   10.95

TOUCHWOOD by Karin Kallmaker. 240 pp. Loving, May/
December romance.   ISBN 0-941483-76-2   9.95

COP OUT by Claire McNab. 208 pp. 4th Carol Ashton Mystery.
                  ISBN 0-941483-84-3   10.95

THE BEVERLY MALIBU by Katherine V. Forrest. 288 pp. 3rd
Kate Delafield Mystery.   ISBN 0-941483-48-7   11.95

THE PROVIDENCE FILE by Amanda Kyle Williams. 256 pp.
2nd Madison McGuire Mystery.   ISBN 0-941483-92-4   8.95

I LEFT MY HEART by Jaye Maiman. 320 pp. 1st Robin Miller
Mystery.   ISBN 0-941483-72-X   10.95

THE PRICE OF SALT by Patricia Highsmith (writing as Claire
Morgan). 288 pp. Classic lesbian novel, first issued in 1952 . . .
acknowledged by its author under her own, very famous, name.
                  ISBN 1-56280-003-5   10.95

SIDE BY SIDE by Isabel Miller. 256 pp. From beloved author of
Patience and Sarah.   ISBN 0-941483-77-0   10.95

STAYING POWER: LONG TERM LESBIAN COUPLES by
Susan E. Johnson. 352 pp. Joys of coupledom. ISBN 0-941-483-75-4   14.95

SLICK by Camarin Grae. 304 pp. Exotic, erotic adventure.
                  ISBN 0-941483-74-6   9.95

NINTH LIFE by Lauren Wright Douglas. 256 pp. 2nd Caitlin
Reece Mystery.   ISBN 0-941483-50-9   9.95

PLAYERS by Robbi Sommers. 192 pp. Sizzling, erotic novel.
                                              ISBN 0-941483-73-8   9.95

MURDER AT RED ROOK RANCH by Dorothy Tell. 224 pp.
1st Poppy Dillworth Mystery.   ISBN 0-941483-80-0   8.95

A ROOM FULL OF WOMEN by Elisabeth Nonas. 256 pp.
Contemporary Lesbian lives.   ISBN 0-941483-69-X   9.95

THEME FOR DIVERSE INSTRUMENTS by Jane Rule. 208 pp.
Powerful romantic lesbian stories.   ISBN 0-941483-63-0   8.95

CLUB 12 by Amanda Kyle Williams. 288 pp. Espionage thriller
featuring a lesbian agent!   ISBN 0-941483-64-9   9.95

DEATH DOWN UNDER by Claire McNab. 240 pp. 3rd Carol
Ashton Mystery.   ISBN 0-941483-39-8   10.95

MONTANA FEATHERS by Penny Hayes. 256 pp. Vivian and
Elizabeth find love in frontier Montana.   ISBN 0-941483-61-4   9.95

LIFESTYLES by Jackie Calhoun. 224 pp. Contemporary Lesbian
lives and loves.   ISBN 0-941483-57-6   10.95

WILDERNESS TREK by Dorothy Tell. 192 pp. Six women on
vacation learning "new" skills.   ISBN 0-941483-60-6   8.95

MURDER BY THE BOOK by Pat Welch. 256 pp. 1st Helen
Black Mystery.   ISBN 0-941483-59-2   9.95

THERE'S SOMETHING I'VE BEEN MEANING TO TELL YOU
Ed. by Loralee MacPike. 288 pp. Gay men and lesbians coming out
to their children.   ISBN 0-941483-44-4   9.95

LIFTING BELLY by Gertrude Stein. Ed. by Rebecca Mark. 104 pp.
Erotic poetry.   ISBN 0-941483-51-7   10.95

AFTER THE FIRE by Jane Rule. 256 pp. Warm, human novel by
this incomparable author.   ISBN 0-941483-45-2   8.95

PLEASURES by Robbi Sommers. 204 pp. Unprecedented
eroticism.   ISBN 0-941483-49-5   9.95

EDGEWISE by Camarin Grae. 372 pp. Spellbinding
adventure.   ISBN 0-941483-19-3   9.95

FATAL REUNION by Claire McNab. 224 pp. 2nd Carol Ashton
Mystery.   ISBN 0-941483-40-1   10.95

IN EVERY PORT by Karin Kallmaker. 228 pp. Jessica's sexy,
adventuresome travels.   ISBN 0-941483-37-7   10.95

OF LOVE AND GLORY by Evelyn Kennedy. 192 pp. Exciting
WWII romance.   ISBN 0-941483-32-0   10.95

CLICKING STONES by Nancy Tyler Glenn. 288 pp. Love
transcending time.   ISBN 0-941483-31-2   9.95

SOUTH OF THE LINE by Catherine Ennis. 216 pp. Civil War
adventure.   ISBN 0-941483-29-0   8.95

WOMAN PLUS WOMAN by Dolores Klaich. 300 pp. Supurb
Lesbian overview.   ISBN 0-941483-28-2   9.95

THE FINER GRAIN by Denise Ohio. 216 pp. Brilliant young
college lesbian novel.   ISBN 0-941483-11-8   8.95

BEFORE STONEWALL: THE MAKING OF A GAY AND
LESBIAN COMMUNITY by Andrea Weiss & Greta Schiller.
96 pp., 25 illus.   ISBN 0-941483-20-7   7.95

OSTEN'S BAY by Zenobia N. Vole. 204 pp. Sizzling adventure
romance set on Bonaire.   ISBN 0-941483-15-0   8.95

LESSONS IN MURDER by Claire McNab. 216 pp. 1st Carol Ashton
Mystery.   ISBN 0-941483-14-2   10.95

YELLOWTHROAT by Penny Hayes. 240 pp. Margarita, bandit,
kidnaps Julia.   ISBN 0-941483-10-X   8.95

SAPPHISTRY: THE BOOK OF LESBIAN SEXUALITY by
Pat Califia. 3d edition, revised. 208 pp. ISBN 0-941483-24-X   10.95

CHERISHED LOVE by Evelyn Kennedy. 192 pp. Erotic Lesbian
love story.   ISBN 0-941483-08-8   10.95

THE SECRET IN THE BIRD by Camarin Grae. 312 pp. Striking,
psychological suspense novel.   ISBN 0-941483-05-3   8.95

TO THE LIGHTNING by Catherine Ennis. 208 pp. Romantic
Lesbian 'Robinson Crusoe' adventure.   ISBN 0-941483-06-1   8.95

DREAMS AND SWORDS by Katherine V. Forrest. 192 pp.
Romantic, erotic, imaginative stories.   ISBN 0-941483-03-7   10.95

MEMORY BOARD by Jane Rule. 336 pp. Memorable novel
about an aging Lesbian couple.   ISBN 0-941483-02-9   12.95

THE ALWAYS ANONYMOUS BEAST by Lauren Wright Douglas.
224 pp. 1st Caitlin Reece Mystery.
                                          ISBN 0-941483-04-5   8.95

MURDER AT THE NIGHTWOOD BAR by Katherine V. Forrest.
240 pp. 2nd Kate Delafield Mystery.   ISBN 0-930044-92-4   11.95

WINGED DANCER by Camarin Grae. 228 pp. Erotic Lesbian
adventure story.   ISBN 0-930044-88-6   8.95

PAZ by Camarin Grae. 336 pp. Romantic Lesbian adventurer
with the power to change the world.   ISBN 0-930044-89-4   8.95

SOUL SNATCHER by Camarin Grae. 224 pp. A puzzle, an
adventure, a mystery — Lesbian romance.   ISBN 0-930044-90-8   8.95

THE LOVE OF GOOD WOMEN by Isabel Miller. 224 pp.
Long-awaited new novel by the author of the beloved *Patience
and Sarah*.   ISBN 0-930044-81-9   8.95

THE LONG TRAIL by Penny Hayes. 248 pp. Vivid adventures
of two women in love in the old west.   ISBN 0-930044-76-2   8.95

AN EMERGENCE OF GREEN by Katherine V. Forrest. 288
pp. Powerful novel of sexual discovery.   ISBN 0-930044-69-X   11.95

THE LESBIAN PERIODICALS INDEX edited by Claire Potter.
432 pp. Author & subject index.   ISBN 0-930044-74-6   12.95

DESERT OF THE HEART by Jane Rule. 224 pp. A classic;
basis for the movie *Desert Hearts*.   ISBN 0-930044-73-8   10.95

SEX VARIANT WOMEN IN LITERATURE by Jeannette
Howard Foster. 448 pp. Literary history.   ISBN 0-930044-65-7   8.95

A HOT-EYED MODERATE by Jane Rule. 252 pp. Hard-hitting
essays on gay life; writing; art.   ISBN 0-930044-57-6   7.95

AMATEUR CITY by Katherine V. Forrest. 224 pp. 1st Kate
Delafield Mystery.   ISBN 0-930044-55-X   10.95

THE SOPHIE HOROWITZ STORY by Sarah Schulman. 176 pp.
Engaging novel of madcap intrigue.   ISBN 0-930044-54-1   7.95

THE YOUNG IN ONE ANOTHER'S ARMS by Jane Rule.
224 pp. Classic Jane Rule.   ISBN 0-930044-53-3   9.95

AGAINST THE SEASON by Jane Rule. 224 pp. Luminous,
complex novel of interrelationships.   ISBN 0-930044-48-7   8.95

LOVERS IN THE PRESENT AFTERNOON by Kathleen Fleming.
288 pp. A novel about recovery and growth.   ISBN 0-930044-46-0   8.95

CONTRACT WITH THE WORLD by Jane Rule. 340 pp. Power-
ful, panoramic novel of gay life.   ISBN 0-930044-28-2   9.95

THIS IS NOT FOR YOU by Jane Rule. 284 pp. A letter to a
beloved is also an intricate novel.   ISBN 0-930044-25-8   8.95

OUTLANDER by Jane Rule. 207 pp. Short stories and essays by
one of our finest writers.   ISBN 0-930044-17-7   8.95

These are just a few of the many Naiad Press titles — we are the oldest and
largest lesbian/feminist publishing company in the world. We also offer an
enormous selection of lesbian video products. Please request a complete
catalog. We offer personal service; we encourage and welcome direct mail
orders from individuals who have limited access to bookstores carrying our
publications.